Trust Your Name

Tim Tingle

7th Generation
Summertown, Tennessee

Library of Congress Cataloging-in-Publication Data

Names: Tingle, Tim, author.
Title: Trust your name / Tim Tingle.
Description: Summertown, Tennessee : 7th Generation, [2018] | Sequel
    to: A name earned. | Summary: When the Choctaw Nation sponsors
    an all-Indian high school basketball team to compete in a summer
    tournament, the team includes Choctaw Bobby Byington and other
    Indian high school players from Eastern Oklahoma.
Identifiers: LCCN 2018026480 | ISBN 9781939053190 (pbk.)
Subjects: | CYAC: Basketball—Fiction. | Choctaw
    Indians—Fiction. | Indians of North America—Oklahoma—
    Fiction. | Oklahoma—Fiction.
Classification: LCC PZ7.T489 Tr 2018 | DDC [Fic]—dc23
LC record available at https://lccn.loc.gov/2018026480

© 2018 Tim Tingle

Cover design: John Wincek

MIX
Paper from
responsible sources
FSC® C005010

7th Generation
an imprint of Book Publishing Company
PO Box 99, Summertown, TN 38483
888-260-8458
bookpubco.com
nativevoicesbooks.com

ISBN: 978-1-939053-19-0

23 22 21 20 19 18   1 2 3 4 5 6 7 8 9

Contents

To Paige Young
and her Papaw Bill,
both eager readers

CHAPTER 1

Stepping Down the Mountain

There's nothing better than playing for the district high school basketball championship.

Of that I was convinced. But I was wrong. Winning your district championship basketball game, that would be better. And we Panthers came so close, but close is never good enough.

I still believe we could have won if Lloyd Blanton hadn't been hurt. Lloyd's ankle was badly sprained and he could barely walk. He sat with his dad in the stands and watched our chances float away, with one bad pass after another.

With only a few minutes to go, I glanced at Lloyd in the stands. He had his head buried in his hands, and what I saw next was worth the evening. Yes, basketball is important—it saved my life. But if you have to choose between your favorite sport and family, the choice is easy.

Lloyd's dad looked to his son and saw his sadness. He grabbed him around the shoulders and pulled him close. I can't read lips, but whatever he said showed a strong father-son bonding. Something like, "They're missing you, son."

Lloyd gave his dad a smile and nodded, "Thank you."

After the game, we rushed through the handshakes and hurried to our dressing room. Soon Coach Robison entered and we grew quiet.

"Men," he said, "this is not the time for a grand speech about the season we have had, the battles we've won and lost. I want to ask one thing of you as you remember tonight's game, over and over, as I will. Hear me out.

"Blame no one. Every one of you fought and hustled and did everything I asked of you, everything your teammates needed. Blame no one, and when you think basketball, think of the games we won. And when you think of the loss, work to improve so next year our friends and family are celebrating. You are all, my young Panther men, champions in my heart.

"Thank you for allowing me to be your coach."

As he turned to go, he had one more thought, one he had to share. "Panthers," he said, and we all grew quiet and turned our attention to him. "No one will ever truly know why certain things happen, but I would like to share something my Choctaw mother used to say.

The Lord works in mysterious ways, his miracles to perform."

What a miracle worker is our coach, Coach Robison. On a night when we lost our only district title in two decades, he left us smiling.

We dressed quietly and quickly and soon stood on the sidewalk, avoiding fans and friends from school as best we could. Nobody wanted to talk. We weren't very good at handling defeat.

Mom and Dad met me in the parking lot, and Dad asked, "You'll probably want to ride home with Johnny?"

"If that's hoke, Dad," I said.

"Sure, Bobby," Dad said. "Stay strong and we'll see you in a few hours."

My best friend, Cherokee Johnny, had his own car and usually gave me a ride everywhere.

As we walked to his car, Lloyd and his dad were waiting for us.

"Mind if I tag along?" Lloyd asked.

"You know you're always welcome," said Johnny.

"I won't be long," Lloyd said to his dad.

"No worries," Mr. Blanton said. He stepped toward his car, then stopped and slowly turned to face us.

"You gotta admit, Lloyd, we're better now with these two Indians on the team," Mr. Blanton said.

Lloyd looked at Johnny, looked at me, and gave us a quiet smile. "Bet that's something you never thought you'd hear from my dad," he said quietly.

"See you in an hour, son," Mr. Blanton said. "Gives you a little play time."

He knew we weren't going anywhere to "play," but he was giving us time to talk through the game. We hopped in Johnny's car and turned in the direction of Lake Thunderbird.

"Any reason you're driving this way?" I asked.

"Yeah," said Johnny. "I thought you'd want to see if they ever repaired the fence you broke.

Wouldn't want you feeling guilty about that little escapade."

"Whoa," Lloyd said. "Get our minds off the game in a hurry, huh, Johnny."

My thoughts took another step to the past, to the night following my first-ever high school game. I played well, we won, and Dad was thrown out of the gym for showing up stumbling drunk.

He waited for me in the parking lot, and as Johnny and I neared his car, he honked his horn loudly and flew past us, shaking his fist at me.

I grabbed Johnny's car keys and took off after Dad, speeding to Lake Thunderbird, his favorite drinking spot. Dad made it fine, but when I saw him standing by the roadside and tapping his hand to his heart, I lost it.

He was letting me know he loved me!

I let go of the steering wheel and crashed Johnny's car through the fence and into the lake. I came so close to dying, but the real miracle was not my survival. My near-death experience brought our family together, really together for the first time—that was the real miracle.

"The Lord works in mysterious ways, his miracles to perform," that's what Coach said.

Johnny parked his car at the roadside park overlooking the lake. The wire fence was now a stone wall. We drank Cokes and DPs, ate chips, and talked about the game. And the past year. Lloyd had an even tougher time than I did.

His dad had survived a heart attack that almost killed him, and why? Because Lloyd refused to give up, caused a ruckus in the hospital, and the doctors gave it one more try.

There followed a beautiful quiet moment, with the moon shining on the lake and waves washing gently against the cliffs. Our minds were a single cloud, floating from one brush with death to the other.

"You Indians sure know how to attack," Lloyd said, "especially when a man is flat on his back."

"I give up," said Johnny. "What are you talking about?"

"I'm talking about when you two attacked my dad's heart."

What?

"Yeah," said Lloyd. "He did everything he could to hate you Indians, to hate your families, to hate Coach Robison because he was Choctaw. So you went on the warpath."

We waited in silence. We knew this was not a joke—his voice was too serious and he was almost crying.

"Dad broke Coach's window and Coach invited him to speak to the team. Dad cussed about you two even playing on the team, to anybody who would listen.

"And what did you do? You attacked my old man with goodness. You forgave him and worked hard to make me part of the new Panthers, the winning Panthers. Thank you, guys."

I can never think of this night as the night we lost the district basketball title. No, I will forever remember this as the night Johnny and Lloyd and I became brothers.

CHAPTER 2

Best Summer Job Ever

The Monday following the game, Coach Robison called us all together after school. We gathered at the gym and sat on the bleachers, having no idea what was about to happen.

"We've had a good year, men," said Coach Robison. "And I am calling you men rather than boys for a reason." He smiled, glancing at the floor, and when he raised his head to look at us, his basketball team, his eyes beamed with respect. He lifted his palms to the ceiling and continued.

"We did not win the district championship, so I won't call it a great season. But what you men have achieved is so far beyond what anyone expected.

"I know the troubles many of you have overcome just to stay in school and keep your grades up so you can play sports. I have seen you come together as a team, on and off the court. Yes, I am proud to be your coach.

"And here's the good news, men," he said. "The Choctaw Nation has asked me to coach a summer basketball team. The Five Tribes will sponsor the team in a summer league, which leads to a national tournament. Games will be played in Tulsa, Oklahoma City, and Little Rock, Arkansas. The regional tournament will be in Tulsa."

Everyone held their breath and no one said a word. I looked at Johnny—he lowered his head and returned my look. We knew where this was going and hoped no one would be upset about being left out.

"As many of you have already guessed, the team I will be coaching is an all-Indian team, with players from high schools mostly in Eastern Oklahoma."

A loud *whoooosh* circled the dressing room, and the feeling of disappointment was like a heavy fog. Johnny and I had the same thought—

how can we leave these guys home, our Panther teammates?

Coach Robison was ready. "Men," he said, "if it were up to me, you would all be on my team till your grandkids had to help you off the court!"

Hoke, we had to laugh at that!

"Coach, we're never gonna get that old," Johnny said. Cherokee Johnny was the only other Indian on our team.

"No, not the way you drive," said Coach.

When the backslapping and laughter drifted away, he continued. "I accepted this job on one condition," he said. "As players show up to try out for the team, you Panthers will scrimmage with us. You'll play as hard and as clean as you have all season, and help me decide who's on the team."

"How they play against you Panthers will go a long way in determining Bobby and Johnny's teammates. We all want this team, the first Indian team ever in the tournament, to win.

"Any questions?" Coach Robison asked.

"When do we start?" Jimmy asked. He was our senior post player and was already wondering where he might play college basketball.

"In two weeks we'll have our first scrimmage, on a Saturday. Can I see a show of hands? Who wants to play?"

Without hesitation, everyone raised their hands.

"That's what I was hoping for," Coach said.

"Thank you, Coach," we all said, shaking his hand as we hurried to the parking lot full of cars and buses.

"Wow," said Johnny as we stepped into his car. "Did you have any idea we'd be playing ball in the summer?"

"Nope," I said. "I knew we'd hit the court at the park every day, to get out of mowing the lawn and repainting the house, or whatever else our dads have planned."

"Wonder if our folks know anything about this," Johnny said.

"Coach is still on the sidewalk," I said. "Maybe if you swing around and drive real slow, we can ask him."

Johnny circled the street and returned to the parking lot, stopping just behind Coach's car as he was opening the door.

I rolled my window down. "Say, Coach," I said, and before I could even get the question from brain to lips, he had his reply.

"I was wondering what took you two so long. Yes, I called both of your parents at noon today. They are as excited as you are. And you'll both be interested in knowing that your dads had summer jobs lined up for you."

"I don't think 'Thank you, Coach' comes anywhere near close enough," Johnny said.

"You are right there, son. Now, drive careful and I'll see you tomorrow for our first informal after-school workout."

"Still the mind-reader," I added as we pulled away. "You know that is a Choctaw power, don't you, Cherokee Johnny?"

"Yeah, and blocking your jumper when you try driving to the basket, that's a Cherokee power. And don't you forget it."

Our minds were ablaze as we left the school, with questions pouring out as fast as we could form the words.

"Where do you think we'll play?"

"Will there be any players from Indian boarding schools?"

"Where do we stay when we travel? Man, I want to get to the national tournament!"

"Did you watch the Oklahoma state finals last year?" Johnny asked. "Man, that Lakota post man was strong! He muscled his way to the basket and nobody could stop him."

"Oh yeah," I said. "They call him *Mato*, a Lakota word meaning *bear*. His name was Mick Harris, but everybody calls him Mato."

CHAPTER 3

Same Old, Same Old

School went by with nothing exciting happening. Well, that depends on what you mean by exciting, as my Uncle Charley says.

Hoke, bully-girl Heather had long ago picked my next-door neighbor and brilliant student, Faye, as the target for her abuse. But now Faye was tutoring Heather, on orders from the principal. Today, Heather was late and missed the tutoring session.

When Heather finally did show up, midway through first period, she had scratches on her neck and a torn blouse. Faye told me about it at lunch as we forked our thin-cut ham and gravy.

"Heather has been late to school all of her life, I'm guessing," she said. "But this time it was different. Before, she'd hide the scratches, change her blouse, and take all the blame for being late. Now she blamed her stepmother."

"Did her stepmother do that to her?" I asked.

"Oh yes," Faye said. "Things must be worse than ever at home."

"What's next?"

"Heather said she can't live with her stepmother anymore and she's finally decided to do something about it."

"No way she'd rather live in a foster home," I said.

"Maybe we should tell her about your hiding place," said Faye.

"Mystery Lady Faye, the whole world knows about my hiding place."

My hiding place, my underground home.

The coffin-sized hole I dug in my backyard, with the weed-covered door over it. My hiding place when Dad came home drunk, which used to be often. No longer. Dad and Mom are the best parents ever, doing their best to please each other, not themselves.

Heather and Johnny and Lloyd, and even Coach Robison, knew about the hiding place.

They kept the secret till I finally trusted Dad enough to tell him. And our lives changed because of our new friendship.

Not right away, of course, but that's another story.

Faye and I hurried up eating, ran our trays to the kitchen window, and sprinted to the hall.

"I'll find out and let you know about Heather," Faye said.

"See ya after class," I said, waving over my shoulder.

Cherokee Johnny and I were meeting Coach and our teammates after school for our first postseason practice, getting ready for the Indian basketball team tryouts. After the final bell, I walked down the hall to the gym. Faye stood waiting for me at the door.

"Any news on Heather?" I asked.

"Yes, Bobby, and maybe it's good news. Heather has been taken away from her home. Her dad was upset, but didn't make a scene at the police station."

"And her stepmother?"

"She was sentenced to six weeks of community service, and when she screamed 'I'll get that lying . . .' you know, the judge sentenced her to a month in jail."

"I hope Heather never has to see her again."

"I'm sure Heather feels the same way, Bobby."

"So where is Heather?"

"That's the good news. One of her aunts has a daughter who just left for college. And since there's an empty bedroom, she has agreed to let Heather live with her."

"How does Heather's dad feel about that?" I asked.

"From what I hear, he's happy about it. Apparently he never tried to stop his second wife from beating up on Heather, and it's been going on for years."

"How can anybody not care about what happens to their daughter?" I asked, fighting thoughts about my own family past and my mother driving away one summer morning. Driving away and leaving me with my alcoholic dad.

"Bobby," Faye said, "when the cops asked him if he knew about the beatings, he told them he did. 'But at least she stopped beating up on me,' he said."

"Her dad, Heather's dad, knew about the beatings?"

"And he admitted it," said Faye.

"And I thought I'd seen everything. So, Faye, you think this is gonna work?"

"You're the Choctaw mind reader, Bobby. Can't you see into the future?"

So, like I said earlier, school went by with nothing exciting happening.

CHAPTER 4

Mato Arrives

As Johnny and I approached the gym, we saw Coach Robison standing on the sidewalk and talking to three high school guys. A blue van was parked in the lot nearby, with the door still open and the driver waiting.

"They must be here to try out for the Indian basketball team," Johnny said.

"How tall you think that big guy is, Johnny?"

"That's Mato," Johnny said. "He's made the All-State team for the past two seasons, and some say he's the best post player in the state."

Johnny and I got dressed and joined our Panther teammates on the court. In five minutes or less, Coach Robison entered the gym with the three players from the bus. They carried travel bags and were followed by the bus driver, with a cup of coffee in his hand.

"Men," said Coach, "there's the dressing room. Get dressed and join us on the court."

"Yes, sir," they mumbled, disappearing into *our* dressing room. The gym grew suddenly silent. It was almost as if Coach Robison had welcomed the enemy into our home. We all stared at him as he walked to midcourt.

Coach waved us to the bleachers and we sat down and waited. "I know, men," he said, "I didn't expect it either. I can see your reaction on your faces, no need to read your minds. I'm with you. Welcoming players from another school into Panther territory, who saw that coming?"

Coach Robison always knows how to turn dark night into bright day, and he did it again.

"Lloyd," he said, "what should we do now?"

And Lloyd—quiet, soft-spoken Lloyd—was ready.

"Well, Coach, if we are feeling weird seeing these players we have never met, Indian players, enter our gym for a practice, what must they be feeling? They're away from home, hundreds of miles maybe, and they know nobody here. No friends, no kinfolks, maybe not even a single tribal member."

"Wow, I never thought of that," Johnny said, and comments floated around as everyone nodded in agreement.

"Yeah, nice going, Lloyd."

"You're right, they gotta be feeling it worse than us."

"So we got a job to do."

"Yes, we do," said Coach Robison. "No time for a game plan here, just do the right thing. You men know how to do that."

We turned to the dressing room door just in time. Three basketball players, tall, medium, and short, stepped to our court. We all looked to Coach Robison, who gestured to Lloyd.

"Welcome to Pantherland!" Lloyd shouted, hopping down from the stands. We all circled our guests, high-fiving and joking till they smiled and relaxed.

"Let's start with lay-ups, men," Coach finally said.

From the first minute, it was obvious these three players were highly skilled. Johnny laid the ball over the rim on his first lay-up, and right behind him came Mato.

No doubt Mato could slam the ball on a two-handed dunk, but he didn't want to be labeled a show-off on his first tryout. He caught the pass, took two quick steps to the rim, and jumped straight in the air. Johnny was standing by and waiting for the rebound.

"I swear, Bobby," he later told me, "his elbows were above the rim. And that was just on the way up! You could have walked under him without ducking, that's how high he jumped."

After ten minutes Coach blew his whistle. "Jump shots," he shouted. "From the free-throw line, then move out to the three-point line."

Eddie McGhee, one of the other Indian players who arrived on the bus, shot some jumpers from the foul line before settling behind the three-point line. He took a few dribbles and launched a shot from five feet behind the line.

If that goes in I'm outta here, I thought. When the ball bounced high off the back rim, I took a sigh of relief.

Eddie smiled and waved his finger at us. "I almost had you," he said with a smile.

"Don't know what you're talking about," I said, as Lloyd whipped me the ball. I let my first three-pointer fly and it rattled around before dropping through.

"Bobby, that's not nice," said Lloyd, "picking on our guest like that."

"Our guest can hold his own," I said. And in response Eddie nailed three shots in a row, no talk, just two dribbles with his left hand and long set shots through the basket.

"Nice shooting, Eddie," Coach shouted from the other end of the court. "I see you're giving Bobby a lesson on three-pointers," he said with a smile.

"I hear Bobby Byington can hold his own from behind the line," Mato said, loud enough for me to hear.

I waved a "thank you" as Mato caught the ball and sailed above the rim for his first dunk shot in our Panther gym.

"What do you think, Bobby?" Lloyd asked.

"I think Coach is putting together a team that will win some ball games," I replied.

CHAPTER 5

First Time for Everything

Eddie and I kept shooting, but nobody was counting. Soon after, Coach Robison blew his whistle. "Come take a seat boys," he said, pointing to the bench.

"Time for introductions," he said. "Mato, or Mick Harris, is from the Lakota Nation. He'll be a senior next year and will be playing in his first summer league."

What did he just say? We all raised our eyebrows, and looked sideways at each other. He *will* be playing in his first summer league. Did Coach just say that?

"That's right, men," Coach said. "Mato will be playing in his first summer league, and so will Greg Tiger and Eddie McGhee. I've kept up with each of you and I knew without a doubt I wanted you three on our team."

"Yeah!"

"Congratulations!"

"Coach knows what he's doing!"

"What a team you guys are gonna be!"

Even the bus driver, Mr. Bryant, stepped out of Coach's office. "Sounds like something good happened," he said, raising his coffee cup.

"We just made the team," Eddie said. "All of us."

"That is good news!" Mr. Bryant said. "Gonna be some happy parents when they find out."

Coach laughed his friendliest laugh. "Hoke," he said. "Time to get back to work. Let's go full-court basketball, with the starting Indian Five versus the Panthers."

For the first time I can ever remember—and this was certainly a day of first-time evers—Coach Robison turned his back to us and took a seat.

"Hoke, he's kinda leaving it up to us," Eddie said.

"That means man-to-man defense, right?" Mato asked. I waved my arms quickly and gathered my teammates together, so no one else could hear.

"Man-to-man, yes, and let's give 'em a real surprise. As the shot goes up I'll take off to midcourt. Mato, grab the rebound, fire it to me, and I'll hit a trailing Eddie for a three-pointer."

Our three Indian guests, Eddie, Mato, and Greg, threw their hands up in the air and burst out laughing.

"What is going on here?" Eddie said, whispering to me. "Bobby, you're telling me to shoot a three-pointer when I can get a lay-up. Coach will bench me. Forever. Or kick me off the team."

I covered my face so nobody could see me laughing. Our Panther opponents were already crossing midcourt, tossing the ball back and forth. "Trust me," I said. "Coach will have something to say, but he'll be hoke with it."

"I hope so," he said, and we high-fived and turned to play some defense.

Bart, our Panther point guard, was a hard-working player, but dribbling was not his strength. Eddie could have swiped the ball several times, but he let Bart take the first shot.

It banged off the front of the rim, and the break began!

Mato grabbed the rebound, took a quick look, and threw a pass half the length of the court. I caught it twenty feet from the basket and fired a pass to Eddie.

He took one easy dribble and launched his first almost game-time three-pointer.

Higher and higher the ball sailed, spinning in a nice rotation. The basket grew to the size of a backyard hot tub, the cheerleaders froze in midair, the buzzer sounded—the game was at stake—and Eddie's shot split the cords! The crowd went wild and ESPN showed the replay over and over.

Maybe a little overkill, as they say, but that's how I saw it. Back to the for-real world. Every Panther in the gym yelled hoorays, and Coach Robison waited for the cheering to end before blowing his whistle.

WHRRRRrrrr!

Even the newcomers knew they were about to see another side of Coach. "So now you men have seen a perfect example of why I am the coach and you are the players," he said. "Bobby Byington, I'm guessing that was your idea?"

"I just wanted everyone to see what we had already learned at the other end of the court," I said.

"And what's that?"

"Eddie McGhee is one great shooter."

Everyone turned to look at Eddie, who lowered his head and shrugged his shoulders. "I was lucky, that's all," he said. The laughter that followed was a good old-fashioned Choctaw laugh, belly-deep and heartfelt.

"Hoke, men," Coach continued, "as you know I am ready to offer all three of you positions on the team. I'll have the paperwork filled out and your bus driver, Mr. Bryant, can take it to your parents to sign."

Thank you, Coach Robison.

For the next hour we scrimmaged half-court, with man-to-man defense. I thought Johnny set the best picks, but Mato was a boulder when he set a screen. With a shooter like Eddie and picks set by Mato, we'd be tough to guard.

After hustling on every play for an hour, with burning lungs and tired leg muscles, we settled into ten free throws each while Coach did the paperwork in his office.

The conversation with our new teammates went well, relaxed and friendly.

"How'd you guys finish in state?"

"We didn't win, but everybody's coming back next year."

"Were you the only Indian on your team?"

"No, I live in Creek country, so most of our team is Creek."

"And your folks are hoke with you taking the summer off?"

"I wouldn't say hoke, but they're allowing it."

"Not exactly, but they'll be at every game."

"I'll be working after the tournament, that's what dad says."

Two and a half hours went by in a flash, and we soon stood on the sidewalk, saying goodbye to our new best friends, Eddie, Mato, and Greg.

As they stepped on the bus, with Coach Robison by my side, I had to say it. "The Choctaw word for 'good-bye' is *chipisha latchiki*," I said. "It means 'I'll see you later.' Chipisha latchiki."

With big smiles from the windows as the bus pulled away, the three called out, "Chipisha latchiki!"

CHAPTER 6

No Other Option

On the morning walk to school, Faye gave me her "Heather update" report.

"Heather spent her first night with her aunt's family," Faye said. "Nothing official about the living arrangements, of course. Not yet anyway. She gave me a call around ten last night."

"Was she doing hoke?" I asked.

"She opened up to me more than ever," Faye said. "She said she felt safe with her aunt and uncle—and Bobby, she called it her new home—but she also said she felt lonely. She said she never expected to feel lonely, but she did."

"What did you tell her?"

Just then a car pulled to the curb, a door opened, and Heather jumped out!

"Mind if I join you?" she asked.

"I'll run along," I said.

"No, no," Heather shouted. "No way! I don't want to split you two up, the happiest couple in the school."

Faye and I had a hard time not laughing. "So how are things with your aunt?" Faye asked.

"Well, I didn't share everything with you last night. And Bobby," she said, looking back and forth from Faye to me, "I'm going to trust you."

I finger-zipped my mouth shut and Heather laughed. "Hoke," she said, "well here goes. I learned a lot about my stepmother last night. Things I never knew. Her own sister can't stand to be around her. She said if my stepmother ever stepped foot on her property, she would call the police. 'You have a new home here, Heather.' That's what she said."

"Wow," Faye whispered. "Sounds like you weren't the only one to have problems with her."

I wanted to ask Heather why she didn't tell somebody about the beatings, but I knew the answer. Fear. Fear that things would get far worse if you told anyone. And shame. Shame that your home was not normal, like everybody else's.

Then another thought hit me, and I had to ask.

"Heather, what's happening with Lloyd?" Lloyd and Heather had been seeing each other for at least a year, long before her troubles with Faye began.

"I asked him to stay away," Heather said.

"Why? You know he cares about you."

"And I care about him too. I just don't want him involved in my family fights. I told him I'll see him at school, and after school whenever we can."

As we neared the front door to the school, habit took over. "Gotta go!" I shouted, and trotted around the corner, headed to the gym.

Coach Robison was already in his office.

"Come on in, Bobby," he said. "Anything special going on this morning?"

"Not yet," I said. "Well, hoke, something special just happened. Heather walked to school with Faye and me. That's never happened before."

"She doing hoke at her new home?"

"So you knew about that?"

"Everybody in town knows, Bobby. No secrets here. But that's not what you came to talk about, is it?"

"I just wanted to know what's going on with the Indian tryouts."

"What did you think of your new teammates, Bobby?"

"They're strong players, Coach. We didn't play against anybody that good all season long."

"I agree, Bobby. And we've got two more coming this afternoon, so don't be late for practice."

"I'm never late for practice, Coach, you know that. Tell me about the new guys."

"Les Harjo, another Creek, and Ryan MacAlvain, a Choctaw from Oklahoma City."

"Another Choctaw! Is he good, Coach?"

"His dad is Choctaw, Bobby, and his mother is Cherokee, so he's got some height. He's six foot five."

"No way! So he and Lakota will battle for the starting center spot?"

"Why not run a double-post offense, keep 'em both on the court?" Coach asked.

"Wow. Two skyscrapers fighting for my missed three-pointers."

"And I might even ask you to throw the ball inside, give them a chance to score a few times a game, Bobby. They'll be here for this afternoon's practice," Coach said, glancing at his watch. "And you better get to class."

"See you after school," I said on my way out the door.

I dashed from the gym and rounded the corner for the back entrance to the school. I opened the door and was about to enter when I heard it.

A battered-up old Chevy swerved into the parking lot, clipped the fender of a teacher's car, and came to a screeching halt. A thin woman in jeans jumped out, slammed the car door, and strutted across the lot, headed my way. Her eyes were bloodshot and she had a bitter, angry look on her face. Heather's stepmother!

What would Dad do? I thought. *What would Dad do?*

I knew right away what my new dad would say and do. "You protect your friends, son, just like in the No Name story." That's what dad would say.

I shut the door behind myself as quickly as I could and hurried into the nearest classroom. Mrs. Lee, my English teacher, was about to call roll.

"Bobby, what are you doing here?" she asked.

"Please, Mrs. Lee, can you call the office?" I dropped my voice so only she could hear me. "Heather's stepmother is here and she's crazy mad. She just hit a car in the teacher's lot and she's coming through the back door any minute now."

Mrs. Lee didn't hesitate. She grabbed the phone from her desk and speed-dialed the office.

"Please send a security guard to this hallway, ASAP. An unauthorized visitor is here."

"Thank you for trusting me," I said, as she hung up the phone.

"Thank you, Bobby. Now, let's take a look." We were about to leave her class, when Heather's stepmother entered the school. She slammed the door behind herself and screamed, "Heather! I'll get you!"

I'll never be able to explain what happened next. I stepped to the hallway and there she was, furious and frightening. Somehow I knew what to do.

"We are with you," I said, approaching Heather's stepmother. "We are all looking for Heather. She came to school this morning, but left with a boy and drove to the lake. They are probably there now. That's what her friends are saying."

"She thinks she can steal from me and get away with it!" her stepmother yelled. Then she did what I hoped she would do. She turned around, left the school building, and hurried to her car.

Hoke, I had lied to Heather's stepmother, but I saw no other option. I had to protect Heather.

Before she could start her car engine, two police cars appeared, one blocking her from the front, the other from the rear.

The security guard, glancing at the outside cameras, had spotted Heather's stepmother and immediately called the police. Heather's stepmother was already well known to school officials. The security guard then hurried down the hallway and rushed Heather to the front office.

Wait one minute! School is still going on, I realized. I took a deep breath, walked to the office, and explained my part in what had just occurred. The assistant principal, Mr. Northcutt, gave me a permission slip.

"Please excuse Bobby Byington for being tardy. He was performing school business," the note read, and Mr. Northcutt signed it.

In world history class, as the Germans invaded Poland, I tried to keep my mind on anything but Heather's stepmother.

"You must stop worrying about things you can do nothing about." I remember Mom saying that to Dad as we returned from a family picnic, months ago. Dad took Mom's advice, and so did I.

I listened to teachers talk, did a few math problems, and ate lunch at a corner table in the cafeteria with Faye and Lloyd. Faye took charge as we sat down, saying, "Bring it up if you want to, Lloyd, but otherwise we'll keep quiet about it."

"Good idea," said Lloyd.

CHAPTER 7

Miracle Room Comes Through Again

The final bell rang. I tossed my books in my locker and headed to my above-ground safety spot, the gym.

Coach Robison stood under the basket for rebounds while Les Harjo, our new Creek teammate, and Ryan MacAlvain, our newest Choctaw, shot free throws. I watched for a few minutes and was soon joined by my Panther teammates.

Les took two dribbles with his left hand, grabbed the ball, and rocked it back and forth twice on the palm of his right hand. Then he arched a soft shot with a nice follow-through.

Ryan's style was slightly different. He dribbled a few times with his right hand, then let it fly.

Both players shot with confidence and hit at least seven or eight out of every ten shots.

"Not bad," Panther Bart said, walking up behind us. "Has anybody missed yet?"

"Yeah," I said, "they've missed a few. But not many."

Coach blew his whistle and we didn't wait to be told. We hurried to the dressing room and in ten minutes were running up and down the gym in a full-court scrimmage. "Let's try a man-to-man press," Coach shouted, "both teams."

He wanted to see if Les and Ryan could dribble and pass when pressured—and of course they could. Ryan took the ball at midcourt and held it high over his head. Les made a quick cut to the ball and Bart darted after him—just as Les hoped. He cut behind Bart and sprinted to the basket. Ryan threw him a sharp pass and Les dribbled in for a lay-up.

Our scrimmage was short, since Les and Ryan had arrived earlier in the day and were a long way from home. "Do your homework and keep the grades up, Panthers, and I'll see you tomorrow. And let's give some high fives to Choctaw Ryan and Creek Les."

On the drive home Johnny said, "Les Harjo, Ryan MacAlvain, Greg Tiger, Bobby, me, Mato and Eddie McGhee, makes seven. We're over halfway there with our summer league Indian team."

"Twelve players. Wish we had twelve Panthers. We coulda won district," I said.

"From what I hear, we can expect half the football team to try out for basketball next year," Lloyd said. "Nothing builds a team like winning, and we did plenty of that."

"No kidding!" I said. "I played summer ball at the park with a few football players. They're not great dribblers or shooters, but they sure know how to bump you outta the way to get a rebound."

"Panthers, Panthers, go, go, go!" Johnny said, and we all had a good laugh.

"Hoke, now that we've had our funnies, Lloyd, what's up next? With Heather's stepmother."

"Jail time, thirty days," Lloyd said, "and she has a restraining order. If she comes within two hundred feet of Heather, she'll be in for some serious jail time."

"Anybody want some backyard hole time?" I asked.

"Only if you call and let your dad know," Johnny said. "And tell him we smelled nachos when we drove by earlier. Hint, hint."

Lloyd laughed out loud. "You guys are the luckiest dudes in school, you know it?"

Dad came through in a way we never expected.

I gave him a call and he met us in the backyard with six cans of chilled root beer.

"I'm at your service, boys," he said, "you know that. Hop in your man cave and I'll bring you some nachos."

Hoke, Dad is up to something, I thought. *This is tooo much, even for him.* In two minutes he knelt down and passed us a huge plate of melted cheese nachos.

"Want some help closing the door, Dad?" I asked. Hint, hint.

"Hoke, boys, I'll leave you alone. Some gratitude!"

Johnny laughed and Lloyd stood up, saying "Thank you, Mr. Byington. We appreciate all you do."

"Try telling that to them Indian troublemakers!" Dad said.

"So says old man Choctaw," I said. "Love ya, Dad."

"Love ya too, son."

We leaned against the cave walls, munching nachos, sipping root beers, and happy to be buried alive.

"Is Heather staying in town?" Johnny asked, looking at Lloyd.

"Yep," said Lloyd. "I wish her stepmother would leave. Heather will never feel safe till she does."

"Maybe if her stepfather got a job out of town," I said, "maybe then they'd move."

"Fat chance of that," Johnny said.

"You have an idea, don't you?" Lloyd asked.

"Maybe," I said. "Coach Robison has friends all over Oklahoma. And if her stepmother wants to start over, it's not gonna happen in this town. A woman with jail time! No way."

"The cost of moving . . ." mumbled Johnny

"The cost of staying . . ." mumbled Lloyd.

"The cost of calling Coach . . ." mumbled me.

Miracle Room, that's what we should call my underground room, 'cause miracles happen often here.

"Give me two days," I said, "and I'll see what Coach has to say. How about we meet, same time, same place, day after tomorrow?"

"Hoke, gotta go," said Lloyd. "Let me know how it goes with Coach."

"Good luck, Lloyd," Johnny said, pushing the door aside and helping lift Lloyd up and out.

When he climbed back in, Johnny pulled the door over our heads and sighed. "First his dad almost dies, then his girlfriend leaves home."

"And remember what we used to think about Heather?" I asked. "She was the meanest bully we'd ever seen. We wanted *her* to go to jail, the way she treated Faye."

"Show's what we really know about other people."

"Next to nothing."

"I heard somebody calling," said a voice from above.

"Mystery Lady Faye, come join us," Johnny said.

With Johnny's help, she soon joined us.

"Any news about Heather?" I asked.

"Nothing you guys don't know," Faye said.

"Tell her your idea," Johnny said.

"Are you still tutoring Heather?" I asked.

"Yes. Why?"

"I had an idea. Can you ask her, real easylike, if she'd be hoke with her stepmother living somewhere else? Tulsa maybe? Anywhere far enough away that she wouldn't have to worry."

"I think we already know the answer to that one," Faye replied.

"Yeah, but just to be sure."

Faye looked back and forth from Johnny to me.

"Mind telling me the plan?" she asked.

"I'm gonna ask Coach Robison if he can find her father a job somewhere," I said. "Once she gets out of jail, nobody in town will want anything to do with her. She won't be happy here."

"She'll never be happy anywhere," Faye said. "But sure, I'll mention it to Heather."

"We have a meeting with Lloyd at four thirty-five p.m. the day after tomorrow," I said. "Can you join us with Heather's answer?"

"Sure," Faye said, "as long as you've got nachos and root beer."

Another voice from above said, "Thought you'd never ask!"

"Dad, are you listening to everything we say?! What if we have teenage secrets? What if I tell my friends what I really think about you?"

Hoke, that was too much, too real. Dad was insecure since he stopped drinking, always afraid of what people really thought. He did not reply.

"You still there, Dad?"

Dad slid the door aside and handed Faye a plastic plate of fresh nachos.

"Yakoke, Mister Byington," Faye said with a smile.

"You are most welcome. And don't close the door yet. I've got something for you too, Bobby. Give me a minute."

As Dad returned to the house, I leaned back against the wall. "Uh-oh," I said. "Dad's gonna get me back. A bucket of ice cubes, dirty bathtub water, something. He's not letting me get away with what I said."

We didn't have long to wait.

"Here, Bobby," Dad said, kneeling down and handing me a plate of warmed-up cherry fried pies. "Here's something to share with your friends."

When he saw the surprised look on my face, he nodded—and a cool, fatherly grin spread across his face.

"Gotcha, didn't I, Bobby?"

"Yes, you did, Dad. Yes, you did."

I was still whispering *yes, you did* as he returned to the house and we enjoyed the warmth of my new dad.

Early next morning I walked to the gym to speak to Coach Robison. I knew I'd find him drinking coffee and reading the morning newspaper.

"Morning, Coach. Can I bother you for a minute?"

"What's on your mind, Bobby?"

"I wanted to run a plan by you," I said. "It's about Heather's stepmother."

"What's your plan?" Coach asked.

"As long as her stepmother is in town, Heather has no chance of a normal life," I said. "You know people all over the state, business owners, people who hire workers."

Coach read my mind again.

"Let me get this straight, Bobby," he said. "You want me to find a job for Heather's father that will force him to leave town? Am I right?"

"Yes, and Heather's stepmother will move too, once she gets out of jail."

Coach slowly reached for his coffee cup and took a long sip. When he finally spoke, his face had that warm Choctaw glow. "Once again, son, I am proud of you. You want to help Heather, bullying Heather."

"She's changed, Coach. Just like my dad."

"You're right, Bobby. Now, I'll think on your plan, and you better get to class."

"I'm gone, Coach," I said over my shoulder, dashing out the door. "See you at practice!"

CHAPTER 8

Call Your Own Fouls

News on the Heather front quieted down and basketball took over. We met every day after school for a quick hour of shooting drills and full-court scrimmaging. Saturday morning soon arrived and Dad banged on my bedroom door.

"Get outta bed, Bobby," he said. "Today is your first day of practice with the all-Indian basketball team! Aren't you excited?"

"Excited is not the word for it, Dad," I said.

"Well, come on, son! Your pancakes are in the toaster oven and syrup is on the table. Come give your Mommy a good-morning kiss."

"Thanks, Dad, but that's your job."

Soon after breakfast Johnny honked his car horn and drove us to the gym. Coach was already

on the court, and ten—we counted 'em—
ballplayers were warming up at both baskets.

"Hey, Bobby, what took you so long?" Eddie
shouted. We shook hands with Les, Ryan, Greg
Tiger, and Mato and nodded at our newcomers.

"Have a seat," Coach said, waving to the
bleachers. "We'll do the introductions later. Are
you men ready for some full-court five-on-five?"

"Yes, sir!" we said.

"Good. We'll play an eight-minute quarter, and
you call your own fouls. Play clean and remember,
the man you're guarding is a teammate. We play
clean. Always. Understood?"

"Yes, sir!"

"Alright. Newcomers first. Johnny, you
and Greg stand up so they know who you are.
Men, this is Cherokee Johnny and he'll be your
captain for today."

He pointed to his right and said, "Johnny,
that's your goal, and you've got five minutes to
get your team organized. Man-to-man defense
and fast breaks are encouraged."

"Let's go, men," said Johnny.

"You men who already know each other,"
Coach said, "that's your goal to my left."

In the fastest five minutes of my life, Coach blew his whistle, whhrrrrr!, and shouted, "Newcomers, your team has the ball first. Let's go! And remember, call your own fouls."

Call your own fouls.

That took away all complaining and fussing about a bad call. When you foul the player you are guarding, you know it. If you pushed a man under the backboard to get a rebound, you did it on purpose. Call your own foul means you are not getting away with it.

Then another thought struck me.

That's how Dad stopped drinking, how he returned to his family. He called his own foul. He admitted he was wrong—not me, not Mom. Dad raised his hand and called attention to the foul he had committed, and I will never forget the courage he showed in doing it.

As Greg Tiger dribbled slowly across half court, Eddie looked my way and gave me a quick tilt of his head, aiming at the dribbler.

Why is he snapping his head at me? I thought. When he dashed to meet Greg at midcourt, I knew what he was saying.

A half-court press! Brilliant!

They'd never be ready for it. I left my man and hurried to double-team Greg. As he picked up his dribble, Eddie and I waved our arms in his face and made life miserable for this far-from-home Seminole.

"Here!" shouted Johnny, running from the free-throw line for the pass. But Ryan jumped in front of Johnny and intercepted the pass. He threw it downcourt to a speeding Mato, who leapt over the rim and rolled the ball from his palm through the basket.

Double-team when they least expect it! Yeah!

Our Guys 2, Newcomers 0

Coach Robison blew his whistle.

Whhrrrr! He had a big smile on his face and was shaking his head.

"I should have warned you Newcomers," Coach Robison said. "Eddie McGhee and Ryan both played on teams that pressed the whole game, and Mato's been fast-breaking before he could walk."

Nobody on the Newcomers was hanging his head. They high-fived and nodded at each other.

Hoke, you got us. Now it's our turn!

I was hoping to see some regular half-court offense," Coach continued. "I'm hoke with the press, but I'm warning you. The Newcomers will be ready this time around."

"Yeah!" The Newcomers hollered, and they were ready. After a few times down court, both teams looked like they had been playing together forever. We set picks, hit jump shots, nailed a few three-pointers. And nobody pushed or shoved or complained. This game was fun!

As the quarter ended, Mom and Dad climbed the bleachers with Johnny's parents and waved at us.

Coach Robison blew his whistle again and called us to the sideline. "Good clean tough play. The kind I like to see, men. Let's slow it down now. Swap ends of the court, and I want to see a little less sprinting from the basket when a shot goes up.

"Remember, we'll be playing teams made up of all-stars, and you'll need to block out to get the rebound. We don't want any second or third shots."

When Coach speaks, we listen. Everybody pounded the boards and every rebound was contested. Mato got his share, so did Johnny and Ryan, my too-tall Choctaw buddy, and a few fouls were called.

"I hit him!" Les called out, as a Chickasaw Newcomer, Phil Morgan, grabbed his cheekbone in pain.

"Sorry, I didn't mean to do it," Les said.

"No problem," Phil said, stretching and rubbing his jaw. "Thanks for the call-out."

He hit both free throws, and as we ran down court I saw Johnny's dad and mine high-five. They liked this style of clean hard play.

That's another never-before, I thought. *A Cherokee lawyer and a Choctaw high-fiving!*

Thirty minutes later, Coach called us together one final time for the day. "Men, we have a buffet meal for you in the cafeteria. Shower and change—Johnny and Bobby can show you the way. Before you leave the gym, I want you to know this. I am proud of every one of you. You are the players I wanted to coach, and this is an honor for me. We will win, on and off the court, and the Native world will be better because of your efforts."

Wow. I never thought of that.

The Native world will be better because of our efforts? As I turned to go, I saw tears streaming down the cheeks of Dad, Mom, and Johnny's parents too.

"Oh, one more thing," said Coach Robison. He stepped to his office and returned carrying a box of T-shirts. "Practice jerseys," he said. "Now, let's see if any of these will fit. Mato, try this one on." He tossed a light blue T-shirt to our Big Bear Lakota post man.

While Mato pulled his regular jersey over his head and said thank you through the cloth, Coach grabbed another T-shirt.

"Let's see, here's a baby size."

"Not funny, Coach," I said, and everyone laughed and slapped my shoulder as Coach handed me my blue shirt. "How did you know it was yours, Bobby?"

"Uh, let's see, Coach," I said. "Maybe because it has my name on it?"

"A Choctaw who can read!" Johnny shouted, pumping his fist. "News flash!"

More laughter.

Five minutes later we all wore our new T-shirts, light blue with our names on the back and the word "Achukma" in large letters across the front.

"Why do the jerseys say *Achukma*?" Mato asked.

"Bobby," Coach said, "why don't you explain what achukma means?"

"Sure, Coach," I said. "Achukma is the Choctaw word for 'good.' We say it all the time."

"And why would I select Achukma for our team name?" Coach asked.

Eddie spoke first. "If it's like the English word 'good,' achukma has two meanings, and both fit our team."

"Go on," said Coach.

"We are a good team, highly skilled," Eddie said. "And we are also good people, always trying to do what's right."

Coach let the silence hang for a moment. We felt his pride and shared it. *Always trying to do what's right.*

"Now, let's head down to the cafeteria for some food," Coach said.

We followed Coach Robison to the buffet meal, with the bus driver, Mr. Bryant, and our parents not far behind. As we filled our plates with roast beef and gravy, veggies, and plenty of dessert—ice cream and still-warm cherry pie— we waited for Coach to speak before we took our first bite.

He said a quiet prayer and we all joined him in "Amen."

On the way home, Mom said, "Your dad and I have lived all of our lives for this day, Bobby."

What's the big deal? some people might ask. If you spent your life hoping nobody would hurt you or your kids because you were Indian, you would understand.

I still remember driving through a town, maybe thirty miles away, and seeing a sign on a restaurant door: *We Don't Want Indians.* Because *No Indians Allowed* is against the law.

Get it?!

"Guess we'll drive through town real slow," Dad said.

"No reason to break the law," said Mom.

But, hey! Things are different now. We have our all-Indian basketball team, and we are gonna win some games.

CHAPTER 9

Will Summer Ever Get Here?

That night, for the first time in six months, Coach Robison showed up at our house. Mom made a pot of coffee and we all sat on the back patio.

"I've got news about Heather," Coach said. "And Bobby, it's not to be repeated."

I nodded.

"Her dad is blaming the school for everything. He says his wife never hit that teacher's car."

It was hard for me to keep quiet. I was there. I saw what happened. Heather's stepmother smashed her old car into the teacher's sedan and was approaching the back door of the school when the cops arrived.

"But he's only trying to clear her reputation before they leave town," Coach said. "I found him a job, Bobby, a decent-paying job in a factory. So Heather's dad has a choice. He can let his wife serve a full month in jail, three more weeks, or he can pack his things and move to the city."

"Oklahoma City," Dad said.

"And the judge has agreed to cut her sentence by two weeks if she agrees to leave town immediately," said Coach. "A friend of mine, a real estate agent, found them a rental house. It's in an old neighborhood, but clean and safe."

"And Heather?" I asked.

"Heather's aunt will get temporary custody," Coach said, "and the restriction remains. Her stepmother cannot come near her. Ever again."

"You are an amazing man, Coach," Dad said.

Coach smiled and hung his head.

"And humble too," Mom said, patting him on the shoulder. "Would you like to stay for supper?"

"Yakoke, but I should be heading home," Coach said. As he stood up to go, he turned to me.

"Bobby," he said, "our next team practice is Friday. We'll practice for a few hours, and the team is spending the night. A local motel is giving us a big discount in rates, both for the team and a few parents who can get away."

"Can't wait," I said.

"Neither can I, Bobby," Coach said.

To say the week crawled by wouldn't come close, but finally Friday afternoon arrived. Coach started the practice with a shoot-around, a chance for us to get to know each other better. Shooting guards and playmakers gathered at one end, and Eddie started by tossing up a three-pointer several feet behind the line.

We stared and hollered "Whooaaa!" as the ball sailed to the basket and "Yooooo!" when it split the cords. Soon Coach blew his whistle.

"Come have a seat, boys!" he shouted. "Good news! We've got a game tomorrow, with a local high school."

Johnny and I looked at each other with bug-eyes and whispered "Wow." No local high school has a chance against the Achukmas. How is Coach gonna pull this off?

"Southside High from McAlester, at noon tomorrow," Coach said. "And as you Panthers know, they have a tough big man and love to fast-break."

Not exactly local, I thought. And their post player was All-State, a six foot five giant, a real challenge for Mato. Suddenly the mood turned serious. Everyone took a deep breath and leaned in closely. Playtime was over; game time was here. Finally.

CHAPTER 10

Achukma, the Bad, and the Ugly

"What's Bobby so quiet about tonight?" Dad asked at the dinner table. I shrugged my shoulders.

"I'm just being a polite little boy, Dad. Pass me the meatloaf, please."

Dad lifted the meatloaf with his left hand and held it away from me. "Hoke, Dad! I'll tell you. Meatloaf please."

"Let me guess," Dad said. "You're worried if Mato can guard that McAlester All-Stater, Tommy Boyd?"

I made an ugly face and stared at Mom. *See what this old man does to his innocent little boy!*

Mom laughed and shook her head. "I'm not getting between you two," she said.

"Yeah," said Dad. "Who wants to stand between a Mac truck and a tricycle?!"

Dad did it again. He made me laugh, made me relax.

After we cleared the dishes, Dad and I sat on the patio. "Talk about anything you like, Bobby. I'm here to listen." He reached across the table and patted my hand, to let me know he was not joking.

"I know we can beat those guys, Dad," I said. "Nobody's gonna dominate inside. Mato and Boyd will both get their points and rebounds."

Dad waited.

"I just hope we don't have to deal with somebody like Lloyd's dad. His old dad, the one who cussed at us and smashed Coach's window."

"Funny you should mention that," Dad said. "Mom and I will be sitting with Lloyd and his family tomorrow."

I looked up and felt the grin growing across my face. "Think you can make him behave?" I asked.

"Who? Coach Robison?"

Jumping ahead. Game time.

The next morning I rode with Johnny to the game. When we arrived, the parking lot was almost full, with the McAlester school bus, parents' cars, and buses from Native culture centers all over Oklahoma. Fans poured out, stretched, and looked for the nearest restroom.

"Man, would you look at that," Johnny said.

"You'd think it was the championship game."

We looked at each other and both had the same thought. *To many Oklahoma Indians, this is the championship game—the first time ever we can stand in a gym built by and for Nahullos and cheer our Indian heroes with pride.*

The gym wasn't packed, but maybe four hundred fans climbed the bleachers. And even though there were no cheerleaders—after all, this was only a Saturday morning scrimmage—a cheer soon swept the stands.

"'chukma, 'chukma,

Go! Go! Go!

'chukma, 'chukma,

Go! Go! Go!"

"Now that's cool," I said to Ryan, my Choctaw teammate, as we shot lay-ups.

We expected coaches to trade off and do the refereeing, but there were real uniformed referees.

Hoke, I thought. *This is more than just a practice scrimmage. Man, I can't wait!*

After warm-ups, Coach herded us to the bench for that one final go-get-'em talk. But Coach didn't follow us to the bench. He walked to the bench where the McAlester players sat.

Surely Coach isn't gonna cause some trouble?!

The entire gym grew silent.

As if that wasn't strange enough, the McAlester coach walked over to our bench, and shook Coach Robison's hand as they passed the scorer's table.

"What's going on?" Eddie asked.

"Wait and watch," Johnny said.

"Now, men," the opposing coach said, "I am Coach Maniford and I coach the McAlester Bulldogs, as you know. We won this year's state title and we are tough. But so are you. I want you to play the best basketball of your life and do everything you can to send us back home as losers.

"Because losers get better and become winners. And we need to be knocked down a notch. Our pride has taken over and we think we can beat anybody. Let us know we can't. Play clean, play hard, and no complaining to the referees, is that clear? We Bulldogs will do the same, and you are in for a battle. Now, hands together."

We all put our hands on Coach Maniford's and he counted to three. In Choctaw!

Achufa, tuklo, tukchina!

"Yeah!" we cheered, then sprinted to midcourt.

"Wait just a minute!" Coach Maniford shouted. "Come on back, men."

We hurried to the sideline, and Coach Maniford had a big grin on his face. "I just wanted to let you know," he said, "Coach Robison and I will switch back after the tip-off."

We all took a deep breath and let the air flow.

WHoooooo!

"What just happened?" Johnny asked me.

"Coach Robison made a new friend," I said. "I'd give anything to know what he said to the Bulldogs."

We soon found out.

As we scooted in between Bulldogs, waiting for the referee to toss the ball up, every Bulldog turned to his closest Indian opponent, reached out for a handshake, and said, "Nobody gets hurt. Deal? Hard but clean."

We shook hands with respect and the game began.

No injuries, I thought. *Please.*

Mato won the tip and slapped the ball to Eddie, who fired me a pass. I hit Johnny, and he threw it back to Eddie, who launched the first shot of the game, straightaway from the three-point line. The ball bounced high off the backboard, and the race was on!

We sprinted back on defense, but not quick enough. Mato was All-State at the post, but so was Tommy Boyd, the Bulldog center. Boyd set up with his back to the basket, ten feet away on the baseline. When Mato muscled around in front of him, Boyd cut to the basket. He caught a lob pass and banked it in.

Bulldogs 2–Achukmas 0

"Heads up, play hard!" Coach Robison yelled.

Johnny tossed me the inbounds pass and I dribbled up court. I hit Eddie in the corner, and he lobbed it over his man to Mato in the post. Mato faked a turn to his right, and when Boyd left his feet, Mato stepped around him for a slam dunk.

"Payback time!" I shouted, jumping up and tossing my fist to the ceiling. Bad idea.

That gave my man just enough time to dash behind me, catch a long pass, and sink the lay-up.

"Uh oh," I said to myself, then looked at Coach and my teammates. "Sorry guys," I shouted. "No more celebrating!"

"Good idea," said Chris, the Bulldog guard who dashed by me for the score. Chris Curtis.

I looked at him and we shared a smile. "Hey," Chris said, "we're here to learn. I don't mind teaching you."

I nodded, bit my bottom lip, and thought of my theme for the day—*Who's teaching who?*

I didn't have to wait long to use it.

"I gotcha covered," Eddie said as he threw me the inbounds pass. He ran by me and said quietly, "Pick and roll, you do the popping."

It was hard for me not to laugh. *How'd he know popcorn is my favorite junk food?*

As we crossed midcourt, I passed to Eddie, still twenty-five feet from the basket. I set a screen for him, and when his man tried to fight over it, I turned and cut to the basket. But too many big men guarded the lane, so I stepped back. Eddie threw me a bounce pass and I let fly with the soft jumper that got me on this team in the first place. *Please let it go in!*

The crowd OHhhed and AHhhed, then broke into cheers, at least those sitting on our side of the gym did.

" 'chukma, 'chukma,

Go! Go! Go!

'chukma, 'chukma,

Go! Go! Go!"

"You're a quick learner," said my Bulldog buddy Chris, dribbling to the sideline.

Achukmas 3–Bulldogs 2

They led by four at the end of the first quarter, and Coach Robison was pleased. "Good hustle, men. They are state champions, so we knew this wouldn't be an easy game. But we will win. Say that with me," he whispered and gathered us close.

We knelt around him, touching hands to shoulders and knees and forming a circle that we hoped would never be broken.

"We will win," we whispered.

"Now, starters take a seat and Team Newcomer, you take the floor. Let's start off with a tough full-court press. Go for the ball, but no hard fouls. Remember, nobody gets hurt.

"And they will be ready for the press, so don't leave the basket unprotected. Alright, men. Hands together."

We slapped our hands on top of Coach Robison's and made the tallest tree of Indian hands this gym has ever seen. "Achukma!" we shouted.

CHAPTER 11

Zipper-Mouth Night

The Bulldogs stayed with their first team to start the second quarter, as we expected. Coach Robison's strategy was no secret. Press full-court, force them to speed up the game just to get the ball downcourt. And when we grabbed a rebound or when they scored, fast break and throw quick passes to the open man.

Why? The Bulldogs had won a state championship and had an All-State big man. But the Achukmas, the Oklahoma Indians, we had nothing but all-stars on our team. Our second unit, Team Newcomer as Coach called them, was strong too, and often outplayed the starters.

Chris brought the ball downcourt to begin the second quarter, and he dribbled in front of our bench. "Why don't you call out for some pizza, Bobby?" he said. "I'll split it with you at halftime."

Coach Robison covered his mouth with his fist to keep from laughing out loud. Yeah, Chris was funny, but funny on the court, as I was learning, doesn't always work.

Johnny and Chickasaw Phil double-teamed him, trapping him on the sideline. Coach Robison leaned out from the bench and waved his pointed finger at me. I knew what he was saying.

He made a joke and it cost him, Bobby. So keep your mouth shut.

Got it, Coach, I Choctaw-told him, with a nod of my head. *I'm a quick learner.*

Glad I kept quiet. Chris had been trapped before. He bounced the ball off Johnny's knee and out of bounds. "Bulldogs' ball!" the referee shouted, tossing Chris the ball.

Coach left Team Newcomer in for the whole second quarter. They did a great job. Johnny couldn't score over Boyd, but he fought hard for every rebound.

And even Chris tired as we kept up the press. Our team was full of energy and we were eager to show the home crowd, the Native crowd, what we could do. Chickasaw Phil had a great mid-range jump shot.

He had that step-back move, where he drove hard and forced his man to stay low and guard the lane. Then he stopped on a dime and took one quick dribble back before launching a fifteen-foot jumper. He scored eight points in the second quarter, on four-for-six shooting!

Chris tried to guard him, but the step-back is impossible to stop. After his third bucket, Eddie looked down the bench at me and pointed to Phil. "Wonder how long he's on Team Newcomer?"

"I'm thinking he's already outscored both of us," I said. But no jealousy, not even close. We were so happy to see the team Coach Robison had put together. We led by six at the half, a ten-point turnaround.

We knew the second half would be tough, especially since we only had a ten-minute break. "No time to catch your breath," Coach said. "No halftime speeches. You can take a seat if you need to or stay on court for a shoot around. And get ready for a different style of play in the second half. Nobody wants to lose."

The Bulldogs had not lost a game in four months! They hated the thought of that long bus drive home after a loss. Still no dirty play, but no more jokes and no coach-swapping.

Coach Robison stepped over to the Bulldog bench to shake hands with their coach just before tip-off. The two coaches were friendly enough, but not like before.

"Team Achufa, first team" Coach said, "you will start the second half." He held out his hands and we added ours.

"Achukma," he whispered, expecting us to shout to the rooftops, like always. I will never know why we did what we did—our Achukma Indian team—but I will also never forget it. Instead of jumping and shouting and storming the court, we whispered too.

"Achukma."

Almost a prayer of thankfulness that we could be here. Together. Our fans and parents felt it too. They rose in silence and waited for the tip-off.

Mato won the tip and Eddie grabbed it, threw it to me, and I drove hard down the sideline. Two Bulldogs double-teamed me, and with nowhere to go I picked up my dribble. I wasn't expecting a half-court press!

These guys were supposed to be hanging their heads with exhaustion. But they were champions for a reason. My Choctaw buddy Ryan cut from his post position for the ball. I ducked under Bulldog Chris and fired him the pass.

When Chris turned to watch the play, I flew past him and caught the ball. *Lay-up time!*

Or so I thought.

Tommy Boyd thought otherwise. He waited for the ball to leave my hand, and just before it hit the backboard, he slammed it so hard it was like a fast-break outlet pass.

Chris lunged for it with his right hand, flipped it over his shoulder, and drove hard for a lay-up. The over-the-shoulder flip was *so cool*, even our own fans cheered Chris. Following the basket, he ran backwards downcourt and smiled and waved to the crowd.

I glanced at Coach Robison, and even though I knew he was not happy with my turnover, he was very pleased with the welcoming cheers from our parents and fans.

A short while ago, Chris would have had something to say to me, but we both agreed, without saying a word, to keep quiet and let our play speak for itself. As the end of the quarter neared, Eddie and I both caught fire.

I faked a shot, tossed him the ball, and set a pick—still a good twenty feet from the bucket.

No problem, oh no, for Eddie McGhee!
His jumper's in net and it's worth three!

I sang my new song for him four times in the third quarter. I only hit two threes, but add a short jumper from the lane as Eddie and I totaled twenty points!

For the Bulldogs, Boyd took over in the low post. He hit short bank shots with either hand. And while the Achukmas hit threes from long range, Tommy Boyd made his three the old-fashioned way, as the announcers say. He made baskets, was fouled, and hit the free throws.

Mato was benched with four fouls, and Cherokee Johnny couldn't stay up with Bulldog Boyd. There was one play I'll never forget and never expect to see again—not in high school. Boyd caught the ball on the baseline and dribbled once under the basket, stepping around Johnny.

As Johnny lifted his arm to block the shot, Boyd ducked under the backboard and lifted the ball *and* Johnny's arm high over the rim, then brought it down in a strong slam dunk.

Hoke, maybe Johnny's arm stayed pretty much connected to his shoulder, but only because Boyd allowed it. Score at the end of the quarter:

Achukmas 72–Bulldogs 64

"Nice playing, men," Coach said as we joined him on the sidelines, very out of breath but doing our best to hide it. "Newcomers, your turn. Let's drop back on the press and stay with a tough man-to-man defense. Pound the backboards.

"Mato, take Johnny's place. You've got two, three minutes, then Johnny's returning. So don't aim for it, but don't be afraid to get that fifth foul, as long as it's clean and nobody gets hurt. Understood?"

"Yes, sir!" we shouted, then pumped hands as the Newcomers hit the court. Mato earned his fifth foul in the first minute, reaching high to block Boyd's shot and catching him on the arm.

With two minutes to go in the game we were clinging to a five-point lead. Chris had played the entire game and had to be exhausted. But he was as determined as ever.

"That's why they are state champs," Coach Robison later said.

Chris swiped the ball on a careless inbounds pass. He could have driven in for a lay-up, but Johnny was waiting for him. So Chris took a step back and launched a three-pointer from the corner. Swish!

Achukmas 90–Bulldogs 88

A little over a minute to go! We had to score, and Cherokee Johnny was our man. He sprinted to the free-throw line and Les tossed him the ball. Without hesitation, Johnny nailed the midrange jumper.

Thirty seconds on the clock!

Achukmas 92–Bulldogs 88

A three-pointer wouldn't be enough for them to pull ahead. We just had to play tough defense and make them earn a bucket.

"Tommy Boyd, ball's going to Boyd," I said, joining Coach Robison and my teammates as we stood up off the bench.

"Just don't foul," shouted Coach, but nobody heard him. The gym rocked with noise, and this was only a scrimmage!

Suddenly the Bulldog coach, Coach Maniford, leapt to the scorer's table and called a timeout. The gym quieted down, but everybody stayed on their feet.

CHAPTER 12

A Star Is Born

Smart move to call a timeout, I thought. *They need a score and a quick steal or a foul.*

Wrong again. Coach Maniford left his players waiting on the sideline and waved to Coach Robison. They talked for a few minutes till a referee blew his whistle for play to begin.

Coach Robison nodded his head up and down, with the biggest smile across his face. He spoke to the referees and before he returned to our bench, he grabbed Coach Maniford by both shoulders.

I don't know what they said but they sure looked like brothers to me. Still standing, the crowd grew silent. A new Bulldog ran to the scorer's table. He bounced when he ran, wore thick eyeglasses, and his shoulders were hunched up around his neck.

"Don't stare, men. You have a chance to be part of something great tonight, something life changing. Here's the plan, and please let us make this work.

"The young man checking in is the Bulldogs' biggest fan. He is a special ed student and unable to play, but he shows up at every practice and his parents take him to every game.

"Coach Maniford even bought him a jersey and he sometimes joins the team on the bench. He has never played, but he works hard on his shot every afternoon after school.

"This game never was about winning, not tonight. That comes later. But tonight Sammy Darnell will be the big winner. Johnny, I want you to back away and let Boyd hit a lay-up."

"Yes, sir," Johnny said.

"Then step out of bounds and toss the ball to Sammy. He'll be ready to intercept your pass under the basket. Let him keep shooting till he scores. Grab the rebound when he misses and hand it to him. Understand?"

"Yes," we all said.

"When he scores, the buzzer will sound and the game will be over. It will end in a tie. Everybody goes home happy."

"And Sammy gets the game ball," Eddie said.

"That's the idea," said Coach. We joined hands and whispered "Achukma," as the Indians and Bulldogs took the court.

The crowd soon saw what was happening. Chris tossed the ball into Boyd, Johnny backed away, and Boyd banked in his lay-up, bringing the Bulldogs to within two.

Achukmas 92–Bulldogs 90

When Johnny caught the ball and stepped out of bounds, Sammy Darnell—special Sammy—hurried after him. He waved his arms back and forth, like in a full-court press. Johnny tossed the inbounds ball to Sammy, who grabbed the ball with both hands and looked back and forth.

When he saw nobody was guarding him, Sammy leaned over, stared at the ball, and took two slow dribbles. Then he lifted his head to the basket and took his first shot. It rolled off the rim, and Johnny snatched it and gave it back to Sammy.

With the crowd cheering his every move, Sammy grinned and jumped up and down after every shot. On the fourth shot, when the ball dropped through the net, he fist-pumped with both hands and ran to the Bulldog bench. The buzzer sounded and the game was over!

The crowd gave Sammy a loud and heart-felt standing ovation. I glanced at Mom and Dad, and they both were wiping their eyes. *More than one life was changed tonight,* I thought.

As we made our way through the crowd to the locker room, Coach Maniford caught up with us. He shook hands with Coach Robison.

"Thank you, Coach," he said, "and give my thanks to your young men as well. This is a night Sammy will remember for the rest of his life."

CHAPTER 13

Two O'Clock, Tulsa Time

On the way home after the game, I asked Dad, "What was your favorite play of the game? How about Eddie's three-pointers? Is he good or what!"

Dad didn't say anything. Mom looked at him and ran her fingers across the back of his neck. "Can you guess, Bobby?" she asked.

"Oh yeah," I whispered. I leaned forward from the back seat and said something I know I should say more often. "I love you, Dad. Sammy's basket, that was your favorite play tonight, wasn't it?"

"Yes, Bobby. To see your team fight so hard the whole game, but when it mattered, you realized that it's only a game. Everyone there won tonight, Bobby. Everyone—we all won."

Dad woke me up early Sunday morning, knocking on the door. "Bobby, the day always goes better if you rise before the sun! Time to get up."

We had a breakfast of pancakes and Choctaw-style blackberry pudding, with a few slices of bacon apiece.

"We thought we'd go to the early service, this morning," Mom said. "It's been awhile since we sang those old Choctaw hymns. Sound good, Bobby?"

"Yes, Mom, good idea."

"Time to give thanks," Dad said.

After church, Dad and I walked a few blocks to the outside basketball court, something we hadn't done in months. We both tried dribbling the ball on the crooked old sidewalk. Not easy.

We shot free throws, jumpers, and mostly just enjoyed a quiet afternoon. On the way home Dad asked, "How's Heather doing, son?"

"She seems hoke, Dad."

"Will you promise to let me know if anything changes?"

We shook hands and sealed the deal.

Monday came too soon, and Johnny and I met Coach in his office before school started.

"Welcome home, men," Coach said, looking up from his laptop. "I've got your summer tournament schedule. Here's a copy for you, and I'm sending email attachments to the parents."

"When do we start?" Johnny asked.

"Our first game is in two weeks," Coach said. "Think we'll be ready?"

"Any more games like the one Saturday?" I asked.

"No, just full-court scrimmages against ourselves. We'll have Friday evening and Saturday morning practices, then tournament play begins. Our first game is two weeks away, two o'clock in Tulsa."

Johnny and I waited and listened. We knew Coach had more to say or we'd already be on the court shooting free throws. He took a deep breath before speaking.

"What I saw Saturday morning makes me think we can win in Oklahoma, win the Midwest, and get to the national tournament."

Johnny and I looked at each other. We knew we were preparing for the summer of a lifetime.

If only we had known.

The school year had finally come down to a matter of days. "Count 'em on on your fingers," Heather said at the lunch table on Tuesday. "Eight more to go."

"Then what happens?" asked Lloyd.

"You buy me popcorn at the basketball games and I share it with Faye," said Heather.

"And I show my bald head again," Faye replied.

"And I climb into my hole," I said.

"And I grow a few inches," Johnny said.

The next Saturday morning Coach had a big-screen TV set up in the meeting room. "The brackets are all set, men," he said. "Our first opponent is a team from Little Rock, the Hawks. They're a first-year team like we are, and the players are the best in the area."

He clicked on the remote and the screen lit up with a film of the Hawks. "Have a seat and let's get to know the players you'll be guarding. Their post man, Drake Weller, can shoot right or left, and also has a nice fade-away from ten feet out. He's your man to guard, Mato, so watch closely."

So this is how the college teams get ready, I thought.

We studied the Hawks for almost an hour, as Coach stopped the film for question-and-answer time.

"Hoke," he finally said, "are you men ready to hit the court?" We were ready. And eager, though nobody said what we were all thinking.

We can beat these guys.

We soon had our chance.

At eight o'clock Thursday morning we climbed on the bus for Tulsa. "We should be there by ten thirty," Coach said. "Rest up, men. We win today and we'll have a game tomorrow night, and hopefully two games Saturday."

Mom and Dad had already claimed their seats when we came out for our shoot-around. Faye and Heather soon showed up, and we had maybe four hundred fans. It was way different watching the Hawks warm up. We whispered their names and talked to ourselves about them.

"Eddie, I wonder if they studied us?" I asked.

"Probably didn't think they needed to," Eddie said.

"Yeah," Johnny said. "Indians can't shoot anything but buffalo."

We were so anxious and excited and ready to play.

"Gimme your hands," Coach said. "Play clean, play hard, and nobody gets hurt."

We joined hands, gave it our team whisper, then shouted "Yeah!" and ran to the circle for tip-off. The Hawks got the tip and right away threw the ball to Drake Weller. He jumped high for the ball, but Mato slapped it away.

Les grabbed the loose ball, fired it to me, and I drove hard to the basket. Two men moved to stop me, so I pulled the old Eddie trick. I tossed the ball over my shoulder to a trailing Eddie, who caught the ball and took his two easy dribbles.

I looked at Coach and pumped my fist as the ball sailed high and straight through the net!

Achukmas 3–Hawks 0

Coach waved his finger at me and gave me his one-eyed glare, Choctaw-saying, *no time to celebrate yet!*

By the end of the first quarter we led 20–12. Weller had scored eight of their twelve points.

"Mato, how're you feeling?" Coach asked.

"Fine, Coach. I'll do better guarding him."

"You're doing fine," Coach said. "They expect us to double-team him, which gets other players open. But you're guarding him one-on-one and doing great. That's why we have the lead, Mato."

Midway in the second quarter we got a cool surprise. Les Harjo, our Creek wing player, felt the magic. It started with a fifteen-footer from the baseline, a wide-open jump shot. When Weller missed a bank shot and Mato tossed me the ball, there was Les again.

Another fifteen-footer, nothing but net! As the first half ended, he'd scored ten points and was five for six from the field.

Achukmas 36–Hawks 22

"They'll come out strong in the second half, men," Coach said. "Ryan, you think a Choctaw can guard Weller?"

"I'll give it a try," Ryan said.

"Good. Mato, you switch men with Ryan. Since Weller isn't dominating like they expected, they'll look to go elsewhere, so be ready."

So be ready.

How could we ever be ready for what happened?

CHAPTER 14

On the Side of Good

When power post man Drake Weller saw Ryan, a smaller player, guarding him, he backed up close to the basket. He caught the ball, stomped his pivot foot close to Ryan and swung around, pounding his shoulder into Ryan's chest. Ryan fell hard on his back.

The referee blew his whistle and everyone waited.

"Charge, number twenty-four," the ref shouted, pointing to Weller and reaching for the ball. Mato helped Ryan to his feet, and Coach stood up and spread his arms wide, letting us know to keep our seats and stay calm.

I looked at Johnny and he nodded. We both knew what an important moment this was for us as a basketball team—as a family of Indian players.

"He flopped!" Weller shouted, holding the ball away from the referee. The ref turned to the Hawk bench for support.

Didn't happen. The Hawk coach was running down the sideline and pounding his fist in his palm. "He was told to flop!" he said. "That's why he's guarding him!"

Now it was our turn to settle Coach Robison. Suddenly a familiar voice sailed over us and tapped Coach on the shoulder. "Need some help, Coach?"

Coach Robison turned around and there was Mr. Blanton, and right beside him stood Lloyd. "Doctor says I should avoid stress, with my heart and all, but I'll take the risk for you!"

Coach Robison gave him the funniest and happiest look of confusion I've ever seen. Then he looked at Dad and Mom.

"You could have warned me," he said to Dad.

"Naw, you woulda called the cops," Dad said, joking, and Mom pinched him on the arm.

Coach turned back to the game. *Fun time over*, he Choctaw-said. *Let's see what the refs are gonna do.*

The referees called both coaches to the scorer's table. The Hawk coach was still hollering as he approached the referees.

We looked over his shoulder and saw a policeman step into the gym. "Coach," I said, nodding at the policeman, "maybe Weller has a history." Coach turned around and took a deep breath. "Will this ever be over?" he asked.

Only just beginning.

Seeing the policeman, the Hawk coach settled down, but kept that angry look on his face. The officer called the referees aside.

"It's your call," he said to the refs. "If you want me to take anyone out of the gym, just say so. Players, fans, coaches; it's your call."

'Thank you, Officer," said the head referee. "We're fine for now."

"I'm here if you need me," the police officer said.

The head ref spoke quietly, and I could see he was giving a warning to the Hawk coach. Then he stepped to center court and said in a loud voice, "Technical foul on number twenty-four of the Hawks. Achukmas, one free throw and take the ball out of bounds."

Coach tapped Eddie on the shoulder for the free throw. He hit it and Coach called time-out.

"Hoke, men, we have our first big challenge," he said. And that's *all* he said, as he waited for us to respond. We looked at each other and the feeling of respect for Coach was strong.

We joined hands and said it—like an old Indian elder's prayer. "Play clean, play hard, and nobody gets hurt."

The Hawk coach took Weller out of the game and the fans behind the Hawks bench booooed! Dad leaned over so we could hear him, but no one else could.

"I am so proud to be on this side of the gym," he said, "with Coach Robison and you young men."

"Yakoke, Dad," I said.

"Thank you," my teammates said, each in their own Native language.

I tossed the ball to Eddie and the game began again. "Let's play," Eddie said as he crossed midcourt.

I knew exactly what he was saying. I ran along the sideline, then cut hard to the top of the circle. Eddie set a pick for me, as I knew he would.

The man guarding me bumped into the screen, and Eddie flipped me the ball. Now wide open, I launched the three.

"If anybody ever doubted that the Achukmas were on the side of good," Dad later said, "all doubts flew out the door when your three-pointer flew through the net, Bobby."

Dad has a way with words.

CHAPTER 15

Makeover and Matthews

Without Drake Weller, the Hawks seemed lost. They had no one to run their offense around, and no big stopper on defense. But their biggest enemy was attitude.

"Men," Coach said as we began the final quarter, "always remember what you're seeing. Teams have lost their best players for years. It happens all the time, at every level—college and the NBA.

"How you respond to trouble, that's what separates champions from everyone else."

The Hawks had no shot blocker in the lane, and Les got an easy bank shot. "No more!" shouted the Hawk coach, and his players knew what he meant.

The next time we had the ball, I threw it in to Ryan. He faked left, then pivoted to his right for an under-the-basket lay-up. Before he could shoot, a Hawk defender shoved him out of bounds!

The referee blew his whistle and ran to the scorer's table as he called the foul.

"Shooting foul on number eighteen, Hawks. Two shots."

He handed the ball to Ryan and we took our places around the lane. Coach Robison eased his palms down, reminding us to stay cool. Ryan made both free throws and the Hawk coach called a timeout.

As we approached our bench, Coach Robison motioned for us to take a seat. "Men," he said, "today is more than a game. I want you to watch what our rival coach does and tell me what you've learned about him."

We knew to be very quiet, but right away Johnny said, "I can already tell you about him, Coach."

Coach smiled and tapped his lips with his finger.

Johnny hushed. What's the right word for what we next witnessed? Makeover?

The Hawk coach made no complaints. He didn't shout and run to the referees. He stood up and motioned to the Hawk who shoved Ryan. He pointed to a seat at the end of the bench. Then he tipped his finger to his head and nodded at the head referee.

"Now, Johnny," Coach asked, "what have you learned.

"Wow," whispered Johnny. "There's good in everybody."

Weller checked in at the scorer's table and the game continued, with no hard fouls and nobody hurt. When the buzzer sounded, we lined up to shake hands with the Hawks. We kept our happy feelings in a tight bundle and hurried through the line.

As soon as we entered the locker room, Coach said, "Hoke, men, I am as happy as you are. But no yelling or cheering. They'd take it as taunting and we don't need any more enemies."

"You mean Indians have enemies?" Johnny asked.

"Whatever gave you that idea?" said Dad, stepping through the door with that big Choctaw grin on his face and slapping Coach on the back.

"Don't worry, Coach," he said. "The post office must have lost my invitation, but I knew you'd want me here."

"Couldn't get by without you," Coach said.

"Yeah, especially after Dad's makeover!" I added.

"I just wanted to let you know how proud I am of all of you," Dad said, heading out the door.

"So," Coach said, "we've got no films on tomorrow's opponent. But better than that, we'll get to see them play. So hurry up, get dressed, and join me in the stands. Game starts soon."

"And we play the winner, right, Coach?" Eddie asked.

"That's right, so let's stay together. And remember, watch the man you'll be guarding; watch what he does without the ball."

We arrived back at the court as the teams were finishing their warm-ups. We sat behind the scorer's table, so we could get a good look at both teams. It didn't take long to spot the best team—the Downtowners, all-star players from the Oklahoma City area.

"Hoke," Ryan said, "who gets to guard that guy?"

A confident guard, over six feet tall, was circling the three-point line, catching the ball and popping long jumpers.

"No more relaxing on defense," Eddie said. "Look at those shooters!"

"You have never relaxed on defense in your life," Mato said.

"No need to start now," Coach said. "That's Riley Matthews, and he's first team All-State."

By halftime the Downtowners led by eighteen points, and it could have been worse. Riley Matthews hit his first three shots and scored ten points in the first quarter. Their post players were muscled up and controlled the backboards, but rarely tried to score.

"Any thoughts?" Coach asked at halftime.

"They play a slow game," Les said.

"I think we can outrun 'em, Coach," said Eddie.

"If they ever miss a shot," I said.

"And if I can ever get a rebound," said Mato.

"So are you boys ready to toss in the towel, head home?" Coach asked.

"No way!"

"Not even close."

"Hey, they aren't scoring against *our* defense."

"I'm believing we can take 'em," Johnny said. "Matthews is taller, but let's see him shoot over Eddie."

"I'd love to see you block his shot, Eddie," I said.

Eddie stayed quiet during the banter, and I knew he was thinking about how to guard Matthews. Finally he leaned over to me and whispered, "If we can stop Matthews we can beat these guys."

The game ended with the Downtowners on top, 57–32. "A convincing win," Coach said. "Ready for some pizza?"

Coach ordered pizza for us all, and we gathered in the dining room of the hotel. He set up his stand and chalkboard and while we munched, he talked.

"How do you beat a slow team?" he asked.

"You outrun 'em!" Eddie shouted.

Coach Robison raised his eyebrows.

"Oh, wait," said Eddie. "Running away after the shot is taken won't work against every team. You have to get a rebound before you can fast-break."

Coach nodded, but said nothing.

"Every Panther fights for the rebound," I said. "Even guards. Everybody. We crash the boards."

"But first?" asked Coach.

"We block out our man so he can't grab the rebound," Les said.

"And then?" Coach asked.

"Then the fun begins," said Eddie. "Mato outruns their big man and Bobby dashes downcourt. I toss the ball to Bobby, he throws it high to the rim, and Mato catches it for a slam dunk!"

Coach waited for the laughter to settle.

"Hoke men," he asked, "should I draw that play on the board or does everybody get it?"

Soft laughter this time, and Coach continued. "We have to rebound and keep Matthews from his favorite shooting spot. Where's that, Eddie?"

"He likes to catch the ball at the top of the three-point circle," Eddie said.

"And then, Bobby?" Coach asked.

"He takes one dribble to his right, and if he is open, he shoots."

Coach turned to Eddie.

"And if he's not open, he passes the ball to the post man at the free-throw line. Sometimes

Matthews cuts to his left, catches the return pass, and shoots."

"Mato," Coach asked, "what happens after the shot?"

"Everybody goes for the rebound," Mato said.

"Not everybody," said Eddie, and I nodded in agreement. "Matthews stays around the three-point line. If they get the offensive rebound, they pass it to him."

Twenty minutes later, when plates were empty and every slice of pizza gone, Coach closed the conversation.

"If we can stop Matthews, we can beat these guys."

Just like Eddie said.

CHAPTER 16

Wake-Up Call

Everybody went to bed early after some in-room hotel TV time. "Bedtime by eleven!" Coach ordered.

I was wide awake at five o'clock in the morning. "You up yet?" I asked my roommate Eddie.

"Yeah, sure. I've been shooting three-pointers," he said, rolling over and burying his head in his pillow.

Suddenly the phone rang! I reached for it, knocked it to the floor, and searched around till I found it.

"Hello?" I asked, hoping there was no emergency.

"This is room service. Did you order pancakes with raspberry syrup and four slices of bacon?"

"That's not funny, Dad," I said.

"I tried to stop him," Mom said in the background.

"Yeah, Dad, go ahead and bring me those pancakes. With bacon and orange juice. Extra syrup. And make that two plates. Eddie is rooming here with me."

"Hey," Eddie said, "it's too early for breakfast."

"It's only my dad," I said, making sure Dad heard me. "He won't talk with food in his mouth, so Mom always serves a big breakfast."

"Very funny," Dad said.

"Yakoke, Dad. I'm learning."

We rolled over and went back to sleep till six. I carried my syrup-loaded plate of pancakes to Mom and Dad's table in the dining room.

"Mind if I join you?" I asked.

"That will be fine, Bobby," Mom said. "And no worries. I already disciplined your dad."

Dad stuck his bottom lip out, pouting. "She's mean to me," he said.

"Oh, poor little Daddy," I said. "If we win tonight, will that make you happy?"

Dad straightened up and looked at me with a bright beam in his eyes. "Yes, Bobby," he said, "that will make me happy. And you *can* beat those Downtowners. Forget about Mark, Luke, and John. You stop Matthews and you'll win."

Mom looked at me. I looked at Mom, and we nodded in agreement.

Not bad, Old Man. Not bad at all.

"We've got the gym from nine to ten thirty this morning," Coach said, walking from table to table. "Be in the lobby by eight thirty and we'll drive over."

"Save your energy for tonight," Coach said as we took the court. "Start with some lay-ups."

Five minutes later he blew his whistle. *Whrrrr!*

"Hoke, men, jump shots, still nice and easy."

Les, Eddie, Ryan, and I walked downcourt, tossing the ball back and forth. When I reached the three-point line, Eddie caught the ball and turned to us.

"Will you guys do something for me?" Eddie asked. "I want to try something out."

"Sure," we agreed.

"Great," he said. "Bobby, you hang out around the three-point line. Maybe just to the left of center."

He wants me to go to Matthews' favorite spot, I thought, but I didn't say it.

"And Ryan, will you play low post, and Les high post?" he asked.

We shrugged our shoulders and did as we were told. I looked at Coach Robison. He was watching us out of the corner of his eye, making no big deal about it.

"Bobby, dribble across midcourt and toss the ball to Les at the free-throw line. Then Les, throw it back to Bobby. And I'm gonna play easygoing defense on Bobby. No pressure."

"You want me to shoot a three-pointer?" I asked. *Like Matthews does,* I thought.

"You got it," Eddie said.

Weird, but I trusted him. *Dumb me!*

So I tossed the ball to Les and he threw it back to me. Eddie stepped away from me, leaving me wide open for the three-pointer.

Or so I thought! He turned back to me as I lifted the ball, taking that sweet, soft jumper.

Eddie took one step in my direction, then planted his foot hard and soared high, way high. As the ball left my hand, he swatted it and the ball sailed to the bleachers, forty feet away.

"Hoke," Eddie shouted. "No more me being boss, men. Back to the shoot-around." He ran to the bleachers and retrieved the ball.

Fifteen minutes later we practiced our defense. "We're only doing a walk-through," Coach said. "Save your energy till tonight."

Soon we piled into the bus and headed back to the hotel. "We'll meet in the lobby at noon," Coach said, "and get some lunch. Hang out around here till then, and no going on the warpath. We'll have plenty of time for that tonight."

After lunch at a fancy burger joint, we spent another long and boring afternoon. Finally, bus driver Mr. Bryant greeted us in the lobby with a big smile.

"Achukmas, let's go win a ball game!"

We piled on the bus and five minutes later (or so it seemed) we piled on the court—warm-up over, tip-off to begin.

"Fight hard for every rebound," Coach said. "Eddie, you'll be guarding Matthews. And remember, play clean and hard and nobody gets hurt."

We piled our hands high and shouted "Achukma!"

Mato got the tip as Ryan jumped in front of his man for the ball. He tossed it to me, and right away I saw where this game was going.

Matthews was guarding Eddie!

Couldn't ask for anything better than that.

You could read the thought on Matthews face. *Short little Indian Eddie McGhee—can't be hard to guard this guy.* He didn't like defense anyway; Matthews wanted the ball.

Eddie saw the look too, and we knew what to do. I drove hard to my left, then spun around and set a pick for Eddie. Matthews trotted to the basket as Eddie ran behind my screen. I tossed him the ball. *Matthews is too good to fight over a screen*, I thought.

"Yes!" I heard Dad shout, and I knew he was standing and pumping his fists to the ceiling. Dad was right. Eddie's three-pointer hit nothing but net.

Achukmas 3–Downtowners 0

We ran back on defense, and as the Downtowners crossed midcourt, Coach yelled at Eddie.

"Pick him up, Eddie. You can't leave him open!" I glanced over and saw Eddie backing off

Matthews, giving him plenty of shooting space behind the line.

Just like he guarded me this morning, I thought. I was right. What happened next silenced the gym. Even Dad sat down, and Coach Robison called the earliest time-out of his career.

Here's how it played out. The Downtowner's point guard threw the ball to his high post, at the free throw line. Matthews let him know he didn't like it, waving his arms in the air and calling out, "I'm wide open."

The low post threw the ball back to Matthews, who caught it and took his one dribble. *He takes one dribble before shooting,* that's what Eddie had said. But still Eddie stayed several feet away.

"Cover him!" Coach shouted.

Even Matthews looked at Eddie, with a sneer on his face. *Yeah, try covering me,* his look said. Matthews jumped up and got ready to shoot a game tying three-pointer.

That's when Eddie sprang into action. He whipped around and planted his left foot to the hardwood, then launched himself high, higher, and still higher.

"No, Eddie!" I shouted. We didn't need a taunting move, not now, not this early in the game. But Eddie was smarter than us all. He didn't slap the basketball into the bleachers. He barely touched it, but it was enough to send the ball rolling from Matthew's hand and across the court.

Les picked it up and fired it to me. The Downtowners were so stunned they didn't move, and I had a free path to the goal for a lay-up.

Achukmas 5–Downtowners 0

Matthews, who had been fussing at his teammate for not throwing him the ball, had his first shot of the game blocked!

I'm guessing this had never happened before. Coach Robison called a timeout and motioned to clear the bench so we'd be sitting. "One question," Coach said, "and I want the truth. Did you men plan what just happened? Did you plan on baiting Matthews into shooting and left me out of it?"

"No, sir," I said.

"Then why were you yelling for Eddie to stop?" Coach asked.

Nobody said anything for a long moment.

"The truth," Coach said.

"Here's the truth, Coach," Eddie said. "I watched Matthews closely yesterday and I wanted to block his first shot. I practiced it on Bobby. But I told no one, Coach. I promise. That's why Bobby was hollering at me. He didn't want me to send the ball to the bleachers, like I did yesterday."

"I saw you do that yesterday," Coach said, "and I'm glad you didn't swat the ball into the crowd tonight. We might not have gotten out of here alive."

"I'm sorry, Coach. I'll ask you before I try anything like that again."

Coach smiled and touched Eddie on the shoulder. "Nice block, son. Guard him close, and no smart-talking, no matter what he says to you. Let's be the deaf Indian champions, how about it," he said, placing both hands in front of us.

We all joined him and whispered, "Play clean, play hard, and nobody gets hurt. Achukmas."

CHAPTER 17

Bobby Better Score

We saw a different Matthews after that. He scored only seven points in the first half. Johnny fouled him on the arm on one three-point shot, and Matthews hit all three free throws. But he was only two of ten from the field on threes.

Achukmas 28–Downtowners 16

With their leading scorer having an off night, the Downtowners lost it. They complained to the refs on every call. They loafed back on defense, they shoved and pushed and gave us not only the game—they gave us a great lesson.

"You hustle and push yourself, you give it all you got," Coach said in the locker room following the game. "But if your mind isn't sharp and focused, you will never be a champion."

Achukmas 52–Downtowners 34

As Mr. Bryant pulled the bus into the hotel parking lot, Coach stood up and turned to face us. "Men," he said, "get to bed, get some sleep, and we'll talk about tomorrow's opponent after breakfast. I'll see you in the dining room at six thirty. Don't be late."

As we crawled into bed and turned the lights out, I asked Eddie, "What gave you the idea of blocking his shot?"

Eddie didn't say anything for a long time.

"You hoke?"

"Yeah," Eddie finally replied. "I was thinking about how I used to be like him, like Matthews. I thought I was better than everybody, nobody could touch me."

"What happened?"

"Later," Eddie said. "Let's get some sleep. We got two games to win tomorrow."

"Anytime you wanna crawl out of your hole, I'll be glad to listen."

Eddie laughed. "I bet you know all about that hole, with a dad like yours."

You have no idea, I thought.

Breakfast came fast. Dad and Mom were acting like grown-ups, missing home. "I'll be glad to get some onions chopped up in my scrambled eggs," Dad said.

"Maybe room service can do that for you, Dad."

"Behave yourselves, boys," said Mom.

"I've got a prediction, Bobby," Dad said, changing the subject.

"I'm listening."

"Hoke. Since Eddie and Mato have done most of the scoring, the Raiders will focus on stopping those two. You and Ryan will carry the scoring load today. That's my prediction."

The Raiders, our opponents at the two o'clock game, were from Edmund, north of Oklahoma City.

"Did you talk to Coach about this?" I asked.

"Oh, you know how he is," said Dad. "Coach has his own ideas."

"Dad!" I whispered, leaning over the table. "What did Coach say?"

Dad looked one way, then the other, then zipped his mouth shut. I leaned back, smiling. Message delivered. I'll be expected to score this afternoon.

"Maybe we can sneak Johnny into the game, Dad."

Dad smiled and shrugged his shoulders.

Coach's after-breakfast talk was a short one. "They play hard-nosed defense and they've scouted every game. So they'll be looking to stop Mato inside, and Eddie will get some double teams. That will leave Bobby open. Ryan, take more of your midrange jumpers. You two can score, so let's do it.

"On defense, they haven't been pressed yet. Let's open with a full-court press. They like a half-court offense, so let's hit the boards after every shot."

Smart Dad. Talk to Coach and warn his kid.

Mato got the opening tip, and Ryan grabbed the ball and tossed it to Eddie. As soon as he caught the ball, he was surrounded by Raiders, forcing him to pick up his dribble. Eddie faked an overhead pass and ducked under the leaping defenders.

He sent me a hard bounce pass, and suddenly we had a four-on-two fast break. I drove hard to the lane, and when Ryan's man left him to stop my lay-up, I flipped a high pass to Ryan for *his* lay-up.

Achukmas 2–Raiders 0

Every time Eddie crossed midcourt, two defenders double-teamed him. He was still able to work his way around them and fire up a few shots. But Eddie was all about team Achukma. He knew tonight was his night to be the playmaker.

So who took the shots? Who hit the threes?

"Bobby Beeee, going for three!"

At first I felt embarrassed to hear Dad holler this new cheer every time I hit a long shot. But I grew to kinda like it. But I didn't take all the shots, no way.

We had strong inside play too, from that other Choctaw, Ryan MacAlvain. Whenever he caught the ball at the free-throw line, Ryan would turn to pass the ball to Mato. Right away, two, sometimes even three, Raiders dropped back on Mato, giving Ryan plenty of time to fire away and hit that smooth midrange jumper.

Halftime score: Achukmas 28–Raiders 19

The second half went by in a flash, and Coach once again proved he knows this game. The Raiders couldn't handle our full-court press, and by the end of the third quarter they were exhausted and ready for the long trip home.

Eddie and I shared the bench for the final quarter, and though we were thrilled with the victory, we knew this day was far from over.

Final score: Achukmas 52–Raiders 39

"Do you realize that you and Ryan outscored the Raiders by yourselves in the first half?" Dad asked. We were crossing the parking lot on our way to a quick lunch.

"Dad, I don't wanna hear that. We won as a team."

"Son, let your dad be proud of you. Just a little."

"Hoke," I said, "as long as we keep it a secret."

"Sure thing, Bobby. Hey, maybe I can start hollering and pushing you around again? That way no one will ever know how proud I am of you," Dad said, hugging me to him.

"Enough is enough," Mom said. Dad gave me a playful shove and I jumped behind Mom's back.

"Mommy, please, I'm going back to the hole," I said.

And who should drive up as Dad and I relived old times?

Lloyd and his dad pulled into the parking lot. Lloyd rolled the window down. "Please tell me you won," he said. "Please don't tell me we drove all this way and won't get to see you play."

"Hoke," Dad said. "We won't tell you. Anything else you don't want to know?"

"That means they won, Lloyd," his dad said. "When's the next game?"

"Tonight we play for the championship. Game time is seven," I said.

"Come join us for lunch. Coach will be glad to see you, you and Lloyd both," said Dad.

They followed us to a nearby restaurant, where we had a long table and a private room. Right after the salads were served, Mr. Bryant stuck his head through the door and motioned for Coach.

Coach had a serious look on his face when he returned, and Mr. Bryant stood behind him. We looked at Coach and waited.

"Did any of you lose your room keys and ask for another at the front desk?" Coach asked.

We looked back and forth from one end of the table to the other. We all shook our heads and shrugged our shoulders *no.*

"Tell 'em what you told me," Coach said to Mr. Bryant.

Mr. Bryant, who was always shy, stepped forward. "Just a few minutes ago the desk clerk at the hotel asked me if those boys found their jerseys. He also wanted the extra room key."

"When I told him I didn't know any boys lost their jerseys, he seemed confused. He said they had to hurry before the game started, so he gave them a room key. He jotted the room number down."

Mr. Bryant scrambled around in his pocket and pulled out a slip of paper. "Room 124," he said.

"That's our room," I said, "mine and Eddie's."

"Men, finish your lunches. I'll call the hotel and see if we can figure this out. Mr. Byington, can you stay here with the team?"

"Be glad to," Dad said. Then he followed Coach to the door and said quietly, "Sounds like Bobby might be involved in this."

"I'll let you know right away what I find out," Coach said. He was gone less than ten minutes, and when he returned he looked worried. "Let's get back to the hotel. Sounds like two young men, claiming to be teammates of yours, were given a key to your room. Last night, while we were at the game."

"They couldn't have taken our jerseys," Eddie said. "We were wearing 'em."

"They had some reason for wanting to get into your room, and we need to find out what it was," said Coach.

When we arrived at the hotel, two police cars were parked in the lot. When they spotted our bus, they exited the hotel lobby and motioned for the bus driver to stop.

CHAPTER 18

Back Seat Ride

Seeing the police officers approach our bus, Coach stood up and said, "Keep your seats, men."

He stepped from the bus and turned to the officer in charge. "I'm Coach Robison," he said. "What brings you here?"

"We are investigating a robbery, Coach," said the officer. "Two of your boys were seen robbing an all-night grocery store last night."

"That's impossible," Coach said. "We keep a close eye on all our players, and none of them have ever had any run-ins with the law. We were playing basketball till almost ten o'clock last night."

"We were given search warrants, Coach, since we had an eyewitness to the robberies.

And we found this bag tucked away on a shelf in the closet of room 124."

He showed Coach a bag with the Panther logo.

"Looks like a bag from your high school," said the officer. "Do your players have bags like this?"

"Yes," Coach said. "We carry our uniforms in these bags."

"That's my bag," I said to Johnny.

"What's the problem?" asked Coach.

The police officer unzipped the bag and showed Coach what was in it, but we couldn't see. Coach shook his head and said, "Officer, my boys did not steal this money."

"Who is staying in room 124?" the officer asked.

"I need to call an attorney," Coach said.

"Tell the attorney to meet us at the police station," the officer said. "Now, Coach, if you don't tell me who is staying in room 124, we'll take every player on your team to the station for questioning."

"Coach, tell him," I said. "We didn't do this and we'll prove it."

"Are you staying in room 124?" the officer asked me.

"Yes, Officer, that's my room number. And I don't know where you found that bag. It looks like mine, but I couldn't find it, so I stuffed my things in Eddie's bag."

"He's telling the truth, Officer," Eddie said.

"Can I see your bag? And what room are you staying in, son?"

"I'm in room 124 too. Just a minute, I'll get my bag."

He climbed on the bus and soon returned with his shoulder bag. "Here, Officer, take a look. It has Bobby's and my uniforms in it."

"What's in the zip pocket on the back?" the officer asked. He took the bag from Eddie and unzipped the pocket.

"There's nothing there," Eddie replied.

"You call this nothing?" the officer asked, lifting a thick stack of twenty-dollar bills from the pocket. He turned to his fellow policeman, saying, "Let's take them both in. I think we've found our robbers."

"Now wait a minute," Coach said, moving between the officers and us—but only for a moment. He saw he was about to cause more trouble for everyone and stepped aside. Just then, Dad pulled up behind the bus.

"Officer, can you speak to this young man's father?" said Coach. "He needs to know what you are accusing his son of. He can tell you where his son was last night."

The officer looked at his fellow policeman and they both had the same expression. *They won't believe a dad who alibis for his son,* I thought.

"What's going on?" Dad asked. He leapt from his car.

No, Dad, please. Don't make it worse, I thought.

New Dad, Old Dad, which would it be?

Mom knows when it's time to step in, and now was certainly the time. She hurried around the car and took Dad by the arm.

I couldn't hear what she said, but I knew what Old Dad would have done. He would have pushed her away and bumped chests with the officer in charge.

New Dad paused for a brief moment, and that moment changed everything. "Bobby needs you to be strong," Mom said, and everyone heard her.

"Can you wait just a minute?" Dad asked. "Please tell me, what is my son accused of?"

"And you are?" asked the officer.

"I am Mr. Byington, Bobby's father. His mother and I took him to his hotel room last night after the team meal, after the game."

"Did you take him to his room, or did you drop him off at the hotel?" the officer asked.

Dad took a deep breath and glared at the officer. Mom gripped his hand and Dad said, "We saw him enter the lobby on his way to his room."

"Officer!" a voice shouted from across the parking lot. Everyone turned and there stood Mr. Bryant, together with the hotel desk clerk. "Officers, you need to talk to this man. He has some important information."

The officer in charge turned to his partner. "No need for handcuffs," he said, "but we're taking 'em down to the station."

The policeman took Eddie and me by the arms with a firm grip and led us to the car. "Stand up against the car and keep your hands above your heads." He patted us down from head to toe.

"Do you have any knives or anything sharp in your pockets?" he asked.

"No, sir," we both said.

He opened the back door to the police car and took first me—then Eddie—by the shoulder and pushed us into the back seat.

"Do you have to do that?" Coach asked. "These boys are innocent and we will be able to prove it."

The officer ignored Coach and spoke to Mr. Bryant and the hotel clerk. "We are charging these boys with robbery. If you have anything to say, say it at the station. You can follow us there if you like."

"That's my son, Officer!" Dad shouted. "He has never stolen a thing in his life!"

"Follow me and you'll have a chance to prove it," the officer said, closing the door to the patrol car and driving away.

Mom grabbed Dad's arm and pulled him back.

I had never ridden in a police car before— and certainly not as an accused criminal, riding in the back seat with my *fellow criminal*, in the eyes of the law. How can this be happening?

I looked over my shoulder as we pulled away, and what I saw came as no surprise.

"We're gonna be hoke," I said to Eddie. Coach Robison had gathered everyone together, our teammates, Mom, Dad, Mr. Bryant, and the hotel clerk. He was speaking to them all as if they were his team and his responsibility.

"Coach is planning our next move," Eddie said.

Just then another car pulled into the lot, and out stepped Lloyd Blanton and his dad.

"Wow!" I said. "I'd almost forgotten the Blantons are here."

We watched as Mr. Bryant led the team into the hotel lobby, followed by Lloyd and the Blantons.

So Lloyd's dad is now becoming a leader, I thought, *settling our team of Indians down, getting us ready to win the championship.*

"What's up?" Eddie asked.

"Just the most amazing turnaround I've ever seen in my life," I said. "I'll tell you later."

Dad pulled away from the hotel with a carload of passengers, Coach Robison, Mom, and the hotel desk clerk.

CHAPTER 19

Through the Looking Glass

When we arrived, the officer led us into the station, and a man met us as we entered. He wore a suit and looked professional and very familiar with the police station.

"Good to see you, Officer Belton," he said, reaching out his hand for a quick handshake.

"What brings you here?" asked the officer, impatient and not glad to see him.

"I received a call from Coach Robison, and I will be representing these young men."

Eddie and I looked at each other. We were glad to have a lawyer on our side, but surprised that we needed one.

"I am George Webster, a local attorney," he said, greeting us with a friendly nod. "And you are Bobby Byington and Eddie McGhee, I am assuming?"

"I'm Bobby Byington," I said.

"I'm Eddie McGhee."

"Excuse us," Officer Belton said, shoving us both to the front desk.

"One moment, Officer," said Mr. Webster. "I have a right to advise my clients."

"Make it quick."

"Men," lawyer Webster said, "you are not to answer any questions until the hotel desk clerk and your coach arrive. The clerk has information the police officers need to hear."

We nodded, and he looked to Officer Belton.

"Do you have a witness that can identify these young men as the robbers?" Mr. Webster asked.

"That's why they're here," said Officer Belton. "Now, step out of my way."

As Officer Belton grabbed our arms and moved us to the front desk, Mr. Webster said, "I've got your backs, men. Stay calm. You'll be on the basketball court tonight."

Officer Belton turned and did his best to stare him down. But our lawyer didn't budge—he gave a strong and determined look right back at him.

"These young men are innocent," he said, "and they have been framed."

As we waited for the policeman to enter us into the system, I spoke quietly to Eddie. "For the first time in my life," I said, "I feel like a slave must have felt. All we can do is wait and do what we are told. Nobody wants to listen to us."

"And nobody believes us," Eddie added.

Then we both looked at each other without saying a word. Slow smiles crept across our faces as we realized how ridiculous that sounded.

"Hoke," Eddie said, "maybe somebody believes us."

"Yeah, maybe Mom and Dad know we didn't rob a grocery store at midnight."

"Maybe Coach Robison believes us."

"Maybe Mr. Bryant believes us."

We could have gone back and forth for an hour, naming all of our friends and teammates. "We are two lucky dudes," Eddie finally said.

"You call yourselves lucky? I don't know if I'd agree with that," said a voice from behind us. We turned and saw a man in a suit, but his face was stern and Eddie and I both had the same thought.

Hoke, here is someone who does NOT believe us.

"I am the district attorney for the city, and we'll see how lucky you are. The store clerk is about to identify you as the young men who robbed him last night."

"Follow me," Officer Belton said, opening a door and shoving us into a room crowded with four other young men, close to our age. Mr. Webster followed us and touched our shoulders.

"I have to leave you now, but it is very important that you stay calm. Remember, you are honest and hardworking ballplayers. You are not guilty of any crime, and looking guilty is the worst thing you can do."

Officer Belton opened a door to a small room with no windows, nothing but a wooden floor. One by one he pointed at us to step through the door and stand before a one-way glass wall. "Face the glass and stand in front of the numbers on the floor," he said.

We soon stood staring at the glass wall, which reflected us. I knew our lawyer was watching us, and maybe the desk clerk. But who else? The man who was robbed at midnight?

"Number Two, step forward," said the district attorney. I glanced at my feet and saw that I was Number Two. I took two steps forward and waited.

"Now, turn around and hunch your shoulders over," the D.A. said.

Turn around and hunch my shoulders? I thought. *Somebody is trying to see me as the midnight robber.*

I did as I was told.

"Now, step forward, Number Four. Cover your face with your left arm."

There was a short pause and we could hear the district attorney speaking to the witnesses. Then he called out, "Officer Belton, take the men back to the holding cell."

"You heard him," Officer Belton said. "Move!"

Eddie and I followed the other men to a nearby cell and waited. Soon our lawyer appeared, and the grin on his face told us what we hoped to hear. "Let's go, men. 'Definitely not those two,' that's what the store cashier said. You are free to go."

"Are they any closer to catching the guys who tried to frame us?" I asked.

"We can talk about that later. Right now let's get you young men back to your team."

We stepped into the front office of the police station, where Mom and Dad were waiting. "How are you holding up, son?" Dad asked.

"Doing hoke, Dad. That was scary, but we made it hoke."

Mom gave me a big hug and whispered, "I have never been so proud of you, how you handled this craziness."

"And Eddie," Dad said, shaking his hand and gripping him by the shoulder, "did you make Bobby behave?"

"You know that's not an easy job," Eddie said.

Dad and Mom looked at each other, and Coach stepped our way after speaking to the lawyer.

"Did I hear somebody trying to be funny?" he asked.

"Nothing else to do, Coach," said Eddie.

We stopped off at the lawyer's office before returning to the hotel. Once inside, he seated us all on sofas and chairs. "I know you all want some answers," he said, "and I wish I had more. I can tell you this.

"The cashier at the grocery store was the most important witness, Bobby and Eddie. The police and the district attorney were certain he would identify you both right away as the robbers, and they'd whisk you away, charge you with a felony, and you would leave this town not with a basketball championship, but with a prison sentence."

"Are you saying," Coach asked, "that my players were framed because they are playing for the tournament championship?"

"Coach, I know that anti–Indian feelings are something you deal with wherever you go. The fans here have not been as rowdy against you and your team as we feared. But they were warned. The students—and even the parents—were sent strong warnings about the penalties for racist taunts."

"But that doesn't mean they will accept us winning the tournament," Coach said.

"I never thought anyone would go so far as to frame your men for a felony," Mr. Webster said. "I guess I underestimated them."

Dad had been silent until now. "So the cashier said right away that Bobby and Eddie were not the robbers?"

"Yes, and the desk clerk at the hotel agreed. The boys he gave the keys to were taller. They told him they were asked to bring the players their jerseys. They didn't say they were basketball players."

"But that doesn't mean they weren't," Coach said.

I could see his mind sailing through clouds of possibilities—the players who shoved and elbowed and did everything they could to hurt us, the fans and coaches who were furious to lose to a band of Indians.

"So, to wrap this up for now—and it will not be over till we catch the guilty ones—I think I'll turn it over to Coach Robison."

"Thank you for helping my men survive," Coach said, shaking Mr. Webster's hand. "As best we can, men, let's concentrate on the game ahead of us."

"I'm ready for that!" Eddie said.

"Same here," I added.

CHAPTER 20

Back to Business

As Dad drove us back to the hotel, Coach gave Lloyd's dad a call. "Blanton," he said, "can you gather the team in the meeting room? Let them know right away that everything is fine. Bobby and Eddie were not charged with any crimes, and we'll be there soon.

"Also, tell them not to ask Bobby and Eddie questions, not now. Let's forget about the arrests, all of it. We'll go there later, but for now we need to focus on winning our game tonight."

Whatever Mr. Blanton said made Coach smile. "And one other request," Coach said. "Would you mind giving the team one of your speeches, like you did before our game last year? If you recall, we won that game!"

We soon pulled into the lot and hurried to the meeting room. Then I remembered New Dad and how important he was to my life. I turned to him.

"Dad," I said, "I knew that whatever happened, you had my back. I knew you trusted me, and I am proud to be your son."

Dad looked at me with that look, almost like he was about to cry. Then he looked at Mom with a quiet smile and pulled me to him for a good old-fashioned father-son hug. And yeah, Mom joined in, and we shuffled in a circle for a moment, a family of dancers chanting an old Choctaw song.

"Wehohana hey-yah."

"Heylo hay yahay hey yah," Coach Robison sang. "Now, if you Choctaws don't mind, we have a basketball game." He looked at his watch. "In two hours!"

Mom shuffled Dad to their room while Eddie and I followed Coach to the meeting room. I know Coach had warned our teammates, the Achukmas, not to talk about the robbery or what we had gone through. But how could we not celebrate this Indian victory!

When we entered the room, everybody stood up and cheered, "Achukma!"

"Now, down to business, men," Coach said. "Gather 'round close." He popped open his laptop and a film of tonight's opponent flashed across the screen.

"Unlike the teams we've played so far, the Fayetteville Five are versatile. Their low post, Billy Archer, can score either right or left, but mostly he bangs his way to the basket and lays it in. And their high post, Don Sanders, can drive to the bucket or hit a midrange jump shot."

"Their point guard, Jay Nickles, is the best playmaker you'll see all year. He sees the whole court and always seems to find the open man. Bobby, he's your man. Play him tight. Eddie, you've got their wingman, another great shooter, Gary Greenley. He loves corner three-pointers and will sometimes slip behind a pick for a short bank shot. The other wing scores on put-backs and short shots. He's there for his defense.

"Hoke, men, let's watch 'em play and I'll stop the film for questions."

I sat next to Johnny as we watched the film, and he patted me on the knee—not talking about the robbery, but letting me know he was with me all the way.

As soon as the film discussions were over, Coach gathered us all at the end of the room, huddled together like before a game. "Men," he said, "this will be a day many of us will remember for the rest of our lives. If you want to turn darkness into light, as I do, let us," then he paused and took a deep breath, "play clean, play hard, and nobody gets hurt. And let's win this game for Eddie and Bobby."

We slowly reached our hands to his and whispered "Achukma," lifting our palms to the sky.

Yes, we are modern kids, young men, modern Americans, school kids. We are also members of our family nations, our Indian Nations. We are Cherokee, Choctaw, Chickasaw, Seminole, Creek, and Lakota. And when we lift our palms to the sky, we're sending our gratitude to our ancestors, our gone-befores, who sacrificed so much for us.

Back to our rooms for a brief rest. Onto the bus for the short ride. Into the gym, onto the court, then warm-ups, speech, and tip-off time— time flew that fast.

I looked to the stands just before tip-off and saw Mom and Dad standing, nervously waving.

Next to them stood Mr. Bryant. And next to him stood his guest, who I later found out was the cashier from the store that was robbed.

"Why did you even bring him to the game?" I later asked.

"I just had a feeling," he said.

The first half was a battle, and it was soon obvious to all that this game could go down to the final minute. We were evenly matched. Mato held his own with the Fayetteville post man. They each pounded the backboards and had seven or eight rebounds apiece at the half. He outscored Mato, but not by much. Their wingman, Greenley, had ten points on three-of-five shooting from long range.

The real game changer came with four seconds left in the half.

Fayetteville Five 31–Achukmas 29

Greenley missed a shot and Mato grabbed the rebound. "Watch the clock!" Coach shouted. Eddie took the pass from Mato, and I glanced up to see time winding down.

Eddie drove hard to the free-throw line, and when my man took a few steps back, Eddie flipped a pass over his shoulder.

Everybody was caught by surprise but me. I caught the ball, took one sweet dribble, and from a foot beyond the three-point line let it fly.

I knew from the moment the ball left my hand, and I was right. The referees waved the three, our fans stood and cheered, and the half was over.

Achukmas 32–Fayetteville Five 31

But the real game changer was yet to happen.

Long after the game was over, Dad told me the whole story. Here's how it happened.

As my shot dropped through the net, Dad cheered, and so did Mom and so did Mr. Bryant— but the cashier, Mr. Finch, did not. He stood up slowly and pointed to the bleachers on the far side of the gym.

"What are you doing?" Mr. Bryant asked. "Bobby just scored. We have the lead."

Mr. Finch said nothing, just kept pointing, while everybody around him cheered. Bryant elbowed Dad. "I think you need to see this," he said.

"What is it?" Dad asked.

"Finch saw something."

Dad leaned around him and asked Mr. Finch, "What's going on? What did you see?"

Mr. Finch motioned for Dad to sit down, and he covered his mouth before he spoke.

"I spotted the robbers," he said. "They are sitting with the team from Tulsa, the tall boy and the boy sitting next to him. They're the ones who robbed me at the store last night."

"I knew I couldn't tell Coach Robison," Dad said. "You still had a game to play."

"Did you call the cops?" I asked.

"I hurried down from the bleachers, making sure those two boys didn't leave. I followed them to the lobby, where they lined up to buy popcorn and sodas. That's when I saw Officer Belton. He and another officer stood by the door. 'There they are, the two boys who robbed the store and framed my son,' I told him."

"Did he believe you?" I asked.

"Not at first, Bobby. I think he was still angry that you and Eddie weren't still in jail."

"How did you convince him?"

"I didn't have to. Mr. Finch, the cashier, was right behind me. 'I swear to you, Officer, those are the two boys who robbed me,' he said, pointing to them, and that's all it took."

"And we didn't hang around after that," Mom said. "Officer Belton spoke to the Tulsa coach, and I pulled your dad away."

"Their coach was furious," Dad said, "and started making a scene in the lobby. So the other officers pulled him away as Officer Belton asked the two Tulsa players to step outside, and that's where he placed them under arrest."

"I'm glad you said nothing to me," Coach Robison added. "As I told them, we have a game to focus on now. The rest will be dealt with later. How was I to know they'd be spotted at the game?"

CHAPTER 21

Championship on the Line

And what a game it was! Down by only a single point, the Fav-Five turned up their hustle-engine— and so did we. Eddie and I had both hit some three-pointers in the first half, so they guarded us tight.

Eddie was ready!

With the score tied midway through the third quarter, he took over. I saw him looking at me like he wanted the ball. I waited till he reached his favorite spot on the three-point line and tossed it to him.

His defender crouched down and guarded him closely. Eddie didn't dribble—he lifted the ball quickly over his head, faking a shot. When his man left his feet, Eddie drove around him, all the way to the bucket.

The Fav-Five post man took one big step in his direction, and that would have stopped anyone else as short as Eddie. But nobody else that short can jump that high!

Eddie soared over him, all the way to the rim, and rolled the ball off his fingers and into the basket. We never trailed after that. Eddie tossed in some threes, I hit a few, and every Achukma on the floor felt the fire.

Final score: Achukmas 56–Fayetteville Five 49

Following the trophy presentation, we quickly showered and changed. "Let's get to the hotel, where we can celebrate!" Coach shouted.

We gathered in the dining room, trying to make sense out of an unbelievable day. "When the championship was on the line," Coach said, "you stepped up!"

Dad picked up our shiny new trophy and held it high. "Yes, they did, Coach!" he said. "They stepped up to the three-point line."

"And we didn't drive all the way from McAlester to see you finish second," said a man's voice from the door. "Go on in, son," he said, ushering in our biggest fan, Sammy Darnell, wearing his thick glasses and a huge ear-to-ear grin.

"I knew you would win," he said. "You did and I knew it!" Out of the corner of my eye I saw Mom dash out the door.

Where is she going in such a hurry? I thought. In a few minutes she returned with an Achukma jersey. She handed it to Coach and whispered something to him.

"We have another award to present tonight," said Coach, standing up. "This Achukma jersey goes to our number one fan."

We all stood and clapped, then lined up to shake Sammy's hand.

"You young men mean so much to my son, and to me too," his father said. "You guys are champs."

When we settled down at the table once more, our thoughts returned to the Tulsa boys, whose lives would never be the same.

"I hope they've learned a lesson," Dad said.

"They will learn their lesson when they blame themselves for everything that has happened this weekend," Coach said. "Blaming others does nothing but dig your hole deeper."

"And my Bobby climbed out of his hole," Dad said.

"So did we all," said Coach. "So did we all."

But the night was not over yet. The desk clerk pulled Coach aside.

"Mr. Finch, the cashier who was robbed, is here," he said. "He wants to say a few words, if that's hoke."

"Sure, tell him he's welcome," Coach said.

CHAPTER 22

Root Beer Toast

Coach held the door open and Mr. Finch entered, looking to the floor and taking one small step at a time. He was in his sixties, balding, and stood maybe five feet six inches tall, with a plump belly.

He wishes he could be invisible, I thought.

Mr. Finch looked around the room, and when he spotted us he lifted his shoulders and shivered. He turned to Coach with fear in his eyes.

"You'll be fine," Coach said, and led him to our table. Dad offered him a seat, but Mr. Finch shook his head. "I'm only here for a minute," he said. "I've caused enough trouble for you already."

"None of this is your fault," Mom said. "Please, won't you join us?" Mr. Finch settled into the empty chair and took a deep breath.

"I am so sorry," he said, glancing around the table. He hung his head and looked so sad I thought he was going to cry! "I never pointed a finger at your son or his teammate," he said to Dad.

"Mr. Finch," Dad said, "we never blamed you. We knew you would tell the truth, and when you did, you saved these boys' lives. You, Mr. Finch, are a hero. Isn't that right, boys?"

"Yes, sir," I said.

"I've never been so scared and so happy in the same day," Eddie said. "And the happy part was because of you, Mr. Finch."

Mr. Finch leaned back and an almost-smile crossed his face. "Do you mean that?" he asked.

"You bet he means it," Dad said. "Now— and I hate to ask you to relive it—but can you tell us what did happen last night?"

Coach had been standing nearby, listening. But now he grabbed a chair from another table and joined us.

"I'll tell you what I told the police," Mr. Finch said, leaning forward with his arms on the table.

Fear's gone, I thought. *He's been waiting for this!*

"It was a few minutes before midnight, and I was starting to count the cash and total up sales for the day. We close at two a.m., but the only sales after midnight are usually at the gas pumps.

"I didn't see a car pull up, but the beeper on the door let me know somebody had entered the store. Next thing I knew there were two men standing in front of the counter. They wore ski masks that covered every inch of their faces, with holes for their mouths and eyes. And under their jackets they both wore Panther T-shirts.

"That's why they accused us first," I said.

Mr. Finch nodded and continued. "They were hunched and turned sideways so I couldn't see them straight on. The tall boy was light-skinned, looked blonde-haired to me, and his arms hung way long, below his knees.

"The other boy was shorter and he was the one with the gun, a short pistol. 'Give it up, man, if you wanna live,' he said. And it was the way he tossed his head back when he talked, that's how I spotted them at the game. He was so cocky."

"I gave them every bill I had, a full day's sales from noon to midnight. Then I held my hands up and backed away. I just knew they would shoot up the store, and maybe me.

"But they tossed the money in a bag and ran out the door. I sat down on the floor for a few minutes, scared to move. When I was sure they were gone, I called the police."

Coach wrapped his arm around Mr. Finch's shoulder, and now he did cry. He sobbed and shook till Dad brought him a cup of coffee. Mr. Finch wiped his face and stammered, "Thank you."

I glanced at Eddie and his stunned look told me we were having the same thought.

They were accusing us of robbing this old man with a gun and threatening his life.

Dad tapped his fist on the table before he spoke.

"Mr. Finch, we have all faced evil square in the face—last night *and* today. But we were strong, we did what was right, and evil did not win. You are part of our championship day. Will you join us in a toast?"

Mom dropped her jaw and looked at Dad with wide eyes, while Coach hopped from his chair and hurried to the kitchen.

"I will be glad to toast your championship day," Mr. Finch said.

In two minutes Coach stepped from the kitchen with six paper cups filled with ice and a big bottle of root beer.

"Root beer on the rocks!" said Dad. We stood, lifted our glasses, and whispered, "Achukma."

"Do you know what achukma means?" Coach asked. Mr. Finch put his cup on the table and looked every one of us in the eyes.

"Yes, I do know what achukma means," he said. "My mother was Choctaw, and she is smiling from above."

About the Author

Tim Tingle is an Oklahoma Choctaw and an award-winning author and storyteller. Tingle performs a Choctaw story before Chief Batton's State of the Nation Address at every Choctaw Nation Labor Day Festival.

In June 2011, Tingle spoke at the Library of Congress and performed at the Kennedy Center in Washington, DC. From 2011 to 2016, he was featured at Choctaw Days, a celebration at the Smithsonian's National Museum of the American Indian.

Tingle's great-great grandfather, John Carnes, walked the Trail of Tears in 1835. In 1992, Tim retraced the Trail to Choctaw homelands in Mississippi, a journey that inspired his first book, *Walking the Choctaw Road*. Tim's first Pathfinders novel, *Danny Blackgoat: Navajo Prisoner*, was an American Indian Youth Literature Awards Honor Book in 2014.

In 2018, Tingle received the Arrell Gibson Lifetime Achievement Award from the Oklahoma Center for the Book. That same year, *A Name Earned*, the third book in his No Name series for young readers, earned a Kirkus Starred review.

PathFinders novels offer exciting contemporary and historical stories featuring Native teens and written by Native authors. For more information, visit: NativeVoicesBooks.com

Tim Tingle's No Name series is the story of Bobby Byington, a Choctaw teen who is proud to be a starter on his high school basketball team but whose personal life is filled with turmoil. Basketball and friendship are driving forces, as Bobby and his friends deal with parental alcoholism, school bullies, and prejudice.

No Name
978-1-93905-306-0 • $9.95

No More No Name
978-1-93905-317-6 • $9.95

A Name Earned
978-1-939053-18-3 • $9.95

Trust Your Name
978-1-939053-19-0 • $9.95